PRAISE FOR
JACK DASH AND THE
MAGIC FEATHER

arf arf arf arf ARF arf arf ARF
(Scabby earlobes, this book is AMAZING. Don't be a
scaredy sock and read it NOW.)
Opi, aged 10

'Original, brilliant and as funny as a pig on stilts!
Jack Dash is my kind of hero.'
Matt Brown, author of *Compton Valance*

'There's mayhem, there's madness, there's even a pet
sea lion! The world of Jack Dash is great fun!'
Ruth Fitzgerald, author of *Emily Sparkes*

'Thoroughly entertaining, exciting, funny and
imaginative – and I love the use of language
and place names: Brilliant!!'
Giles Andrae, author of *Billy Bonkers*

'It is funny with a captial 'F'!...
Jack Dash and The Magic Feather is a crazy, clever,
carnival ride of a story. Bonkers, brilliant and
feather-tastic! You had me at 'Oi! Dozy Knickers!'
Mo O'Hara, author of *My Big Fat Zombie Goldfish*

JACK DASH
AND THE
MAGIC FEATHER

By
SOPHIE PLOWDEN

Illustrated by
Judy Brown

Catnip
PUBLISHING LTD

FOR MARCUS AND MILO

CATNIP BOOKS
Published by Catnip Publishing Ltd
320 City Road
London
EC1V 2NZ

This edition first published 2015
1 3 5 7 9 10 8 6 4 2

Text copyright © Sophie Plowden, 2015
Illustration copyright © Judy Brown, 2015
Cover design by Pip Johnson

The moral rights of the author and illustrator have been asserted.

A CIP catalogue record for this book is available from the British
Library.

ISBN 978-1-84647-099-8

www.catnippublishing.co.uk

'Everything you can imagine is real'
– Pablo Picasso

ONE

'Oi! Dozy-knickers!'

Jack Dash spun on his heel. *Who said that?* His dark eyes flashed across the back garden, left to right.

'D'you want a Sherbet Slammer?' the voice called again. 'They're extra strong.'

Jack rubbed his ears: it was coming from the hedge. He dropped to the ground and, silent as a mamba, he crawled through the grass.

The hedge rustled.

A-ha. A freckled nose was poking through the leaves: an intruder . . .

an imposter . . . a spy! 'I know you're in there,' he hissed.

The hedge snorted.

'It won't work – I got you surrounded.' As the branches parted, he leaped to his feet. 'Okay – you asked for it. Put your hands on your head and . . .'

Out she climbed: a girl about his age, with stripy trousers and red, curly pigtails. She tugged a twig from her hair, reached into her backpack and thrust a paper bag under his nose. 'Go on,' she said. 'Eat it.'

Jack slid his hand into the bag and pulled out a great, green, glob-oozing nugget. '*Eat* it?' He stared at the girl and he stared at the thing in the palm of his hand: it looked like it lived in an old man's hanky.

'Eat it,' she said. 'If you *dare.*'

It was an alien slug from Planet Yuck and he was supposed to put in his mouth?

'What are you even doing here?' he said. 'This is private property.' He wiped a blob of goo off on to his jeans, folded his arms and glared at her. 'I'm a professional wrestler, you know.'

'Oh yeah?' She was looking him up and down. 'What's your ring name, then?'

'My what?'

'You know, your professional wrestling name.'

'Oh. It's – er – Jumping Jack Dangerous.'

'No, it's not – it's Scaredy Sock.'

'*Scaredy Sock?* Ha!' Jack opened his mouth, tipped back his head and threw the Sherbet Slammer in.

Crunch. He blinked.

Squirt. He coughed.

'Gnnrrgggh.' He grabbed his throat with both hands.

'Hey, your eyes have gone all watery.' She was standing so close their noses were almost touching. 'You're not *crying* are you?'

'Nnnggh.'

'And your face is bright red. Tell you what – I'll cool it down with the high-pressure hose. It goes like a rocket. Wait right there.'

She disappeared into the hedge and, moments later, she clambered out again, dragging a hosepipe through the leaves with the nozzle in her fist and her finger on the trigger. 'My dad'll kill me if he finds out – last time I used this I knocked him off his bike.'

Jack tried to shout out, but his lips had gone numb. *She's dippy. She's daft. She's a half-baked, fully-fried, tonsil-toasting fruitcake.* He began to back away just as The Fruitcake squeezed the trigger.

'You're soaking!' said Mr Dash. 'What on earth's the matter?'

Jack was kneeling on the back doorstep, panting like a poodle. 'My t-t-tongue,' he said. 'It's combusting!' He stumbled indoors and slid the bolt. 'Dad – quick – shut the windows, lock the doors – she's – she's . . .'

'Who? Where? What are you talking about?'

'In the g-garden – freckles and pigtails!'

Mr Dash peered through the glass. 'There's nobody there. Can't you see I'm busy? I've got to polish the crockery and . . . Jack? Where are you going?'

'A weapon!' he cried. 'I need a weapon!' And into the kitchen he sprinted.

'Hello, Jackie darling,' said Mum, who was unpacking boxes on the floor. 'Have you been exploring our new garden?'

'There's a girl out there and she's got these sweets and . . .'

'That's nice . . .' she said, fishing out a potato masher. 'Now, what shall we have for lunch?'

'Nice? *Nice?* She's a carrot-topped criminal – she tried to blast my face off!'

'Did she really? Isn't that lovely?'

'*Lovely?* She's about as lovely as a dentist with his drill switched on and a hornet up his trousers. We can't live here any more – we'll have to move back home.'

'Dumpling, I'm trying to tidy up. Why don't you go and brush your hair?'

Knock-knock-knock

Someone was at the front door.

'That's her,' said Jack, snatching the masher from her hand.

'Don't be a silly sausage – it's the removal men with our furniture.'

'Don't worry Mum, I'll protect you.' He ran into the hall, waving his weapon. 'Dad,' he yelled. 'Wait!'

But his father was already opening the door.

tWo

It's official — this is war. Jack ran up to the attic and slammed the door behind him. So he'd got it wrong this time and waved a potato masher in the removal man's face, but that didn't mean the Fruitcake wasn't coming back. She'd be planning another attack for sure — it was only a matter of minutes . . . *Action Plan Number 1: secure HQ and commence ambush manoeuvres.*

'I'll hide in the duvet — no, under the bed. Then I'll grab her by the ankle and —' *The bed — where's the bed?* He looked left and right. There was no bed. 'I know — I'll launch my stomp-rocket down the stairs and *whee-boom-splat*, she's Marmite!'

But as he squinted into the gloom, the truth struck him like a fork in a sausage: there was no stomp-rocket . . . no spy-kit . . . no car collection . . . and no laser-directed marshmallow-launcher. Everything he owned in the entire universe was in boxes in the kitchen or in the back of a van.

Jack slumped to the floor. *So this is it – my new bedroom – and it looks like no one's been in here since the invention of the cobweb.* He trailed his finger across the dusty floorboards and crinkled up his nose: it smelt of stale biscuits. Cracks ran across the ceiling like the rivers of the Mississippi Delta. At the far end of the room, sunlight fell through the grimy window into a smudgy grid on the floor.

Do Mum and Dad really expect me to sleep in here – all alone – in an attic? And what about the rats? They'll come out at night with their snaggly teeth and their squiggly tails and they'll eat my face and gnaw my bones to powder.

Only that morning he'd begged them not to move. He'd tried everything. Mum was like, *we have to because of Dad's new job and you're overreacting and don't be a silly dumpling* and Dad was like, *I can't take much more of this and I've just about had enough and if you don't unchain your ankle from your bike then I'll strap you to the roof rack.*

Jack hauled himself to his feet and drifted to the far window; he pressed his nose to the grubby glass and gazed across the roof tops – past the pigeons, the chimney pots, the TV aerials and the street lamps – at the houses marching down Quarantine Street below. He sighed. If only he could follow them – all the way out of Curtly Ambrose and back to Maiden Over, to 7 Lancelot Road and his best friend, Neville in number 9. He'd race round and call through the letterbox, 'Ahoy there, Captain Nelly!'

He could see it now: the door opening just a little and Neville's face through the crack. 'Jack-pot? Z'at really you?' He'd grin his crumpled grin and fling the door open. *'No way.* You haven't!'

'Oh yes I have,' Jack would say. 'I've run away.'

'But your mum and dad . . . they'll freak!'

'My mum and dad *are* freaks. All they care about is their stupid new house and Dad's stupid new job and they wouldn't even notice if my head fell off and bounced down the stairs. They'd just tell me to clean up the mess.'

'Jack, this is serious. They'll call the police. They'll print your photo in the newspaper – and – and . . .'

'And they won't find me . . . cos *you're* going to help me out.'

'*Me?* Oh no. No, I can't. Really. I haven't even finished my homework.'

'Listen. I've got it all sorted: I'll hide in your bedroom cupboard, underneath your PE kit. All you have to do is sneak me food when your mum's not looking. Cake and crisps and stuff like that, s'long as it's not Brussels sprouts.'

'You can't live in my bedroom cupboard forever!'

'Won't be forever – just until I grow a beard. What d'you think, Nelly? You and me against the world!' He tapped the window. 'Nelly? . . . You there?'

Of course he wasn't. Neville was twenty four and a half miles away and Jack was alone in an attic, talking to himself. *Who's the fruitcake now?* His lower lip quivered. Alone. Abandoned. Trapped. He wiped his eyes with his scarf and turned away . . .

And that's when he saw it. Funny he hadn't spotted it till now – an old fashioned desk with an inkwell and a lid, tucked in the corner beneath the window. And beside it stood a rickety wooden chair. *Weird. Is there a light on inside it?* He cocked his head – yes, glowing through the gap under the lid. He edged towards it and shivered. It was like someone had opened the freezer compartment and forgotten to shut the door. *Don't open it*, he told himself, even as he lifted the lid.

It was extraordinary.

It was the strangest thing he'd ever seen – stranger than flamingos and aubergines and his mother on a bicycle: the desk blazed like a pirate chest. He raised his arm to shield his eyes: like a pirate chest full of shimmering, sparkling, slightly blinding treasure.

What is it? What's in there? Ten . . . nine . . . eight . . . seven . . . and on the count of zero, he slid his hand inside.

tHREE

Jack lowered himself on to the chair and laid the book on the desk. It was old and heavy and bound in dark green leather . . . and it was shining like a lamp.

There must be a bulb inside.

He turned the cover and coughed as a puff of dust rose into the air − *it can't have been opened for years and years.* He ran his half-chewed fingernail over the ancient paper, over the label on the front page, printed with the words: *This Book Belongs to . . .*

Underneath it, someone had added

a name. He squinted at the scratchy handwriting. He blinked. He swallowed. He wrapped his scarf tight and rubbed his eyes with his fists. Not just any old name . . .

This book belongs to...

JACK DASH

'Scabby earlobes, this is creepy.' Now his heart was drumming in his ribs. 'Who did this?'

He turned the page . . . blank. And the next. And the next. But the glow grew stronger with every page he turned. A-ha! Here was something sandwiched in the centre – not a bulb, but an envelope: long and old and crumpled at the corners and so dazzling it was like staring at the sun. On the front was a message, written in the same spidery handwriting:

I will bring your dreams to life . . . if you know where to draw the line

What was *that* supposed to mean? And there was something inside – he could feel it. He frowned. *Someone's playing a trick on me.* He turned the envelope over. The flap was sealed with red wax. *But who? Is this the work of The Fruitcake?* He bit his lip. *But she doesn't know my name . . .*

'Here goes.' He cracked the seal and
. . . *FLASH-BANG!* – the envelope
sprang from his hand.

Jack dived to the floor with his head in
his arms, ready for the blast. He waited.
And he waited. Was it on a timer? He
raised his head a millimetre and eased
himself to his knees; the envelope lay on
the floorboards, half a metre away. He
shuffled closer.

*Easy now. I dunno what's in there, but it's
definitely dangerous.* He reached out his hand.
Definitely dangerous with a capital D. He lifted
the flap with his outstretched finger and
peeked inside. 'Huh . . . ? It's a *feather.*'

Not an ordinary feather like you'd

find on a pigeon, on the pavement or in the park, but a long, gold, curling feather. *Must be from a very rare bird – like a tufted jay . . . or a spotted spoonbill . . . or a yellow-bellied sapsucker.* He plucked it out and twirled it between his thumb and finger. It glittered with a thousand fiery flashes, lighting the room like a firework in the sky.

Think straight. There's a battery inside it, there has to be. Jack held it to the window and squinted at the shaft. There was no battery. 'I will bring your dreams to life . . .' he murmured. He shook his head. 'No,' he said. 'No way. Feathers don't grant wishes – that's impossible.'

Except . . . he thought, as he tapped its glistening fronds, *it crackles and it flashes and it bangs and isn't that impossible too?*

Like King Arthur with his trusty sword,
Jack raised the feather high above his head.
He coughed. '**OH MIGHTY** . . . feather,'
he said. 'Take me home.' He scrunched his
eyes shut, crossed his fingers and squished
his toes together. And as still as a statue,
forgetting to breathe, he waited.

Hmm . . . Maybe it needs more information.

'Take me back to Lancelot Road. To my bedroom and my car collection and Captain Nelly and – wait! I forgot something.'

He clutched the feather to his heaving heart. '. . . *Please.*'

Jack opened one eye . . . then the other . . . He looked left. He looked right. No zips, no zaps, no Lancelot Road, no Captain Nelly, no nothing. His heart sank like one of Mum's jokes. He hadn't moved a millimetre.

I must be dumber than a deckchair. The feather fell from his hand and landed on the open book.

SPLAT

'That's weird.' Something black and sticky was oozing from its tip. Jack picked the feather up and shook it.

Splat – splat.

Shiny flecks of ink zigzagged up the page. He whirled it over his head, slashing the air like a knight in battle. 'Take that, you scoundrel!'

Splat – splat – splat, till the paper was covered in splodges and smudges and –

'Dumpling?'

Mum! How long had she been standing there, spying at the door? He slammed the feather inside the book and crammed the book into the desk.

'I've brought your things up.' She plonked a box on his bedroom floor and peered inside it. 'Do you really need all this stuff?' she said, dangling a yellow flip-flop in the air. 'And what about these?' Out came a pair of swimming goggles . . . a Viking helmet with a missing horn . . . 'Oh dear, oh dear, oh dear.' She planted her hands on her hips, looked around his bedroom and sighed. 'This room needs a deep dusting! And the delivery men have forgotten to bring your bed so I'll have to unpack your sleeping bag and we've got to go shopping and . . . Jack, look at the state of you!'

But Jack wasn't looking at the state of himself, because something strange was happening inside the desk: he could feel the lid beneath him, chattering like a pair of teeth.

'What's that all over your hands?'

'My hands?' Jack leaned down hard on the lid with his elbow. What was going on in there? Why was it sending shockwaves up his arm and juddering through his jaw? 'It's, um ... n-n-n-n-n-nail varnish,' he said.

'Nail varnish? Well, you haven't applied it very well. And close your mouth, sweetie – you're dribbling all over the furniture.'

'H-h-huh?'

'Come along, Jackie – we've got to go out.' She stopped. She frowned.

Takka-takka-takka

'What's that noise?'

Good question. Jack leaned down harder. What *was* that noise?

Takka-takka-takka. 'There it is again.'

She tilted her ear towards him. 'Sounds like popcorn.'

The lid was hammering his elbow now. **Jiggle-jiggle-jiggle** – he couldn't control his head any more and Mum was advancing towards him.

'Will you please stop dancing, Dumpling!' She waved her finger at the desk. 'What's inside that thing?'

'D-d-don't look!' he said. 'It's a p-p-present . . . for your b-b-birthday.'

'How thoughtful,' she said, 'but it's not for another six months.'

'Dotty!' That was Dad shouting up the stairs.

Mum glanced at the door. 'Now your father's getting cross.'

'Do-teee!'

'Jack,' she said as she headed for the landing, 'we've got to leave. I want you ready by the front door in three minutes.'

'I'm c–c–c–c–coming!' He lunged for the box she'd left on the floor and heaved it up on to the lid of the desk.

FOUR

Drriiiiiing!

Mrs Dash folded her arms and shook her head. 'No,' she said, 'I don't think so, it's not very *friendly*.' She leaned over the counter and beamed at the shop assistant. 'I'm looking for something to match my personality. Something a bit more perky.'

The assistant held up a row of white buttons on a wooden board. 'Try the one at the end,' he said. 'It's our best seller.'

Mum jabbed a button with her forefinger.

Bing – bong!

'Well, that's certainly nice and cheerful. What do you think, Dumpling?'

'Huh?'

'Pay attention, sweetie – I'm choosing a bell for our front door. What about this?'

Ding-a-ling-a-ling!

'Great!' said Jack. 'Can we go now, please?'

She tried another.

Honk-honk!

Nee-naw, nee-naw, nee-naw!

Cock-a-doodle doo! She giggled and pressed it again. *Cock-a-doodle dooooooo!*

Oh no, thought Jack.

'Oh yes,' said Mum. 'It's absolutely perfect. I'll take it. And do you have any party hats?'

Jack ran to the window and looked out across the road: there was his father in the hardware shop, with a can of paint in his hand. *Get a move on, please! I've got a full-scale emergency back in my bedroom!* But Dad was shaking his head. He returned the can to the shelf, picked up another and squinted at the label.

'Dumpling . . . ?' Mum gave a little twirl. 'What do you think?' On her head perched a lilac tiara, studded with silver hearts. 'Isn't it super? I feel just like a princess. Oh, I can't wait to show your father!'

'Come on,' said Jack, wrenching the door open. 'He's right over there in the –'

'Just a moment, sweetie!' Mum turned

back to the assistant. 'Could I try out those doorbells again?'

Jack and his mother staggered to the front door of number 33 Quarantine Street, clutching their shopping bags, while Mr Dash fiddled with the keys and nudged the door open with his elbow.

Mrs Dash stepped inside, dropped her bags on the doormat and froze. The shriek that parted her lips could have split an atom.

'Dotty?' Dad dropped his bags and rushed in after her. 'Are you – goodness gracious, what on earth . . . ?'

'What is it?' said Jack. He ran inside and skidded to a halt. 'Oh my naked armpit!'

A huge, black cloud was humming in the hall.

'Mum?' he gasped. 'Dad? Where are you?' The cloud was alive. Alive with a thousand bluebottles, buzzing and swirling – in his hair, down his ears, on his cheeks, up his nose.

Somewhere in the mist he could hear his mother whimpering, 'Lionel, *do* something!' Then there was the gangly shape of his father, hopping and leaping, all elbows and knees.

'Shoo! Skedaddle! Clear off!' Dad yelled, waving his arms like a windmill.

Jack buried his face in his scarf as a thousand more came billowing down the stairs, coating the walls in a sticky black carpet. **ZOM-ZOM**. Through the door they swept, roaring on to the street, louder and faster than a German motorway. **ZOM-ZOM-ZOMMM** – till Jack thought his eardrums would pop.

And then the hall was empty. Silence. Like when Dad said, 'Bedtime!' and switched the telly off.

'Oh Lionel!' said Mum. 'You're a hero!'

He leaned on the doorframe and coughed. A fly flew out of his mouth.

'I don't understand,' she said, rubbing his back. 'I must've left the kitchen window open.'

No, thought Jack, as he watched them zigzagging over the road. *They didn't come through the window. I saw them — they came from upstairs.*

The cloud was thinning and spreading into the sky like flecks of ink: *splat — splat — splat.* He pictured the book . . . the page . . . the feather in his hand. *Takka-takka-takka —* the noise in the desk . . . And a thought stole over him like a shiver. He slipped back inside, tiptoed past his parents and followed the staircase all the way up to his bedroom in the attic.

'Weird things happen all the time,' Jack told himself. 'It's natural — like rainbows and magnets and waxy ears.' He opened his bedroom door — and heard the drone of a lonely bluebottle skating across the window. 'So? There are insects in my bedroom — doesn't mean it's got anything to do with the . . . huh?'

The desk was lying on its side: its lid was open.

Jack set it back on its feet. And there was the box he'd left on the lid — and all the stuff inside it scattered across the floor. He picked up the book lying open at his feet. He picked up the feather. He drew up the chair and sat down.

Biting his lip, he smoothed the book on

to his knees and flicked a dead fly off the page. There they were in black and white: the splodges that the feather made – *splat* – *splat* – *splat* – zigzagging up the paper. He leaned forward. *Yes.* He tilted his head. *It looks like a swarm of bluebottles.*

'I will bring your dreams to life,' he murmured, 'if you know where to draw the line.'

FIVE

Just as a storm fades and its dark clouds are pierced by a clear, blue sky, Jack was beginning to understand. But was he right? Had the feather really made the ink splats come to life? Did he – Jack Alphonse Exeter Dash – really, truly, actually – *draw* the swarm of flies that was, at this very moment, turning off Quarantine Street and into Vaccine Lane? And if he did, could he do it again? Did the feather grant wishes after all?

Jack reached for the feather. *There's only one way to find out.*

SIX

'This is it,' thought Jack. 'I know exactly what my wish is gonna be.' His fingertips tingled as they gripped the feather. 'Oh wow. I can practically *feel* the magic.' He pressed the tip to the paper. 'So . . . where do I start?' He smiled to himself. 'Easy – I'll draw my bedroom window.' One, two, three, four – he drew the sides of a rectangle. Criss-cross, criss-cross – he divided it up into panes.

'That's the first one – how many more? Hmm . . .' He chewed his lip. 'How many windows does Lancelot Road have?'

Better get this right, he thought, *or I could end up somewhere weird, like Middle Wallop or Woolloomooloo or Tombstone, Arizona.* 'Maybe I'll try the roof . . . if I can remember what it looks like.' He put the feather down and scratched his head. 'Is it flat or pointy?' He scrunched his eyes shut. *Think, think, think.* Bang! He bashed his fist on the desk. 'I don't know!' he wailed. 'I can't remember. And if I can't remember, then how will I ever . . . huh?'

There was something on the page . . . something hard and flat and shiny.

'That positively, definitely wasn't there before.' He picked it up. 'Looks like a bar of chocolate.' ***Snap!*** He broke off a square and popped it in his mouth. 'Mmm . . . tastes like chocolate, too.' He looked at his drawing of the window. He looked at the bar of chocolate. Window. Chocolate. Chocolate. Window. Same shape. Same little squares. He laughed out loud. 'The feather worked. It actually worked – my drawing came to life!'

Jack turned the page over. 'I'll try again and I'll draw something simple . . . something that won't go wrong.' He grabbed the feather and grinned. 'I'll draw a wrestling mask . . . a Jumping Jack Dangerous wrestling mask!'

Slowly, carefully, he drew an oval. He drew two circles inside it for eyeholes. *Now for the best bit.* Zigzag, zigzag – he drew a pattern of flames round the edge.

'Hey – that's cooler than a polar bear's toenails.' He clenched his fist. *Come on feather, do your magic!* He held his breath and –

'Whoa! Who turned the lights out?' Jack felt his face with a pat-pat-pat. 'Yes! I can feel it.' He stretched the mask down over his nose so he could see out through the eyeholes. 'It's a perfect fit! I must be getting the hang of this.' He ran to the box and scrabbled through it. 'There must be a mirror here somewhere.' A sock . . . a shoe . . . a silver car . . . *Hang on,* he thought. *I could draw a toy car! Now why didn't I think of that before?*

Back he ran and flipped the page over. 'I'll add gadgets and gizmos and extra gears and when Neville comes to stay, I'll race his Thrust Bucket on my bedroom floor and I'll thrash it!'

Jack pressed the feather to the paper and with a grin as wide as a bumper, he started: up, along and down he guided the feather-tip. He drew a windscreen and hubcaps, headlights and a pair of fins, a streamlined chassis to minimise drag and one, two, three, four . . . five exhaust pipes bristling at the back. He sketched grooves in the tyres to handle the bends. He added aerials, pedals, buttons and dials.

Something's missing, he thought. *Captain Nelly, of course!* He drew a head and a body and arms and legs and he added a crumpled smile. Then he sat back in his chair.

Ravioli Ultra 700

'Ladies and gentlemen, boys and girls, I present *The Jack Dash 700 Ravioli Ultra* – the fastest racing car in the world!'

He could see the racetrack, the stadium and – whoosh – the chequered flag. *The engines howl, the tyres screech and the crowd roars –*

'JACK!'

Come on feather – you can do it. Bring the car to life! Brm, brmm, brrmmm, two laps of the room and –

'JA-ACK!'

Mum. What did she want now? In The Most Annoying Parent in the World Competition, she'd definitely win the lifetime achievement award.

'DUMPLING!!!!!'

Jack charged across the room, flung the door open and bellowed down the stairs. 'Coming!' He glanced over his shoulder. *Hurry, hurry, hurry,* he begged the feather.

'Surprise!' she called up the stairs. 'Your friend's here to see you!'

I knew it – I knew he'd come. Jack ran out on to the landing. 'Ahoy there, Captain

Nelly – come on up!'

THUD! Behind him. **BANG! BOING!**

Bouncing bisons – what was that? Jack spun around. His mouth dropped open. He rubbed his eyes and took a step closer to his bedroom door. He gasped and turned away. He looked back and gasped again.

'Oo,' he said, like a chimpanzee in a scalding bath. 'Oo – oo – ooo!' It was miraculous. It was mind-blowing. It was magnificent. Even as he started laughing, hot, salty tears were spilling down his cheeks.

SEVEN

'Just wait till Neville sees this.' Jack wiped his eyes and giggled; he was fizzing over like lemonade. It was berserk . . . it was bonkers . . . yet there it was, as plain as porridge: **The Jack Dash 700 Ravioli Ultra** – gleaming in a shaft of sunlight – parked in the middle of his bedroom floor.

He'd never seen a toy car like it. It was longer than a bathtub and the roof came up to his chin. Jack peeped through the passenger window and pinched his arm. This was no dream. 'I'm definitely awake . . . I drew it with the feather and now it's real: one thousand, one hundred and ten per cent real!'

Jack trailed his finger along its silver fin and counted the aerials: seventeen exactly. *Tap-tap-tap*, he knocked on the roof, then peered around the back: one – two – three – four – five exhaust pipes, exactly like his drawing. *I will bring your dreams to life if you know where to . . .*

'Hi there, Parpy Pants – how's your tongue?'

'Neville?' Jack spun around. Disaster. He lunged for the door – too late! A tangerine trainer had wedged it open and a monstrous face was grinning through the gap. *I don't believe it*

— *Mum's finally flipped and let The Fruitcake in.* 'What d'you want?' he said, leaning on the door with the full force of his shoulder.

'I'm Coco McBean. D'you wanna be friends?'

Friends? Is she joking? I'd rather eat toe fluff.

'Neville's my friend. Goodbye.' He gave the door a shove, but now she'd got her elbow through, followed by her knee.

'Ow! That hurts. Stop being annoying and let me in.'

'Annoying! *Annoying?* You're the one who hides in hedges. You're the one who tried to exterminate my taste buds, then blast them off with a high-pressure hose.'

'Lighten up, lemon-face – it was only a joke.' She jammed her face right up to the gap. 'Why are you wearing knickers on your head?'

'It's a wrestling mask. Now go away.'

Like a hungry piranha, she widened her beady eye. 'No, it's not – it's a pair of knickers.'

'How many times do I have to tell you? It's a Jumping Jack Danger—'

'There're pink, they're frilly and they're knickers. And you're wearing them on your head.'

'What?' Jack craned his neck round so he could see into the car's wing mirror.

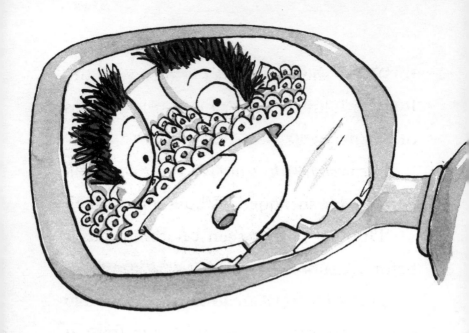

His mouth dropped open. Two
dark eyes blinked back at him,
surrounded by strawberry lace.
He yanked them off and –

Bam! The door flew open. Disaster times
ten: Coco McBean was inside his bedroom.
He'd dropped his guard for a millisecond
and The Fruitcake had forced an entry.

'Well,' she demanded, staring at the Ravioli Ultra with her hands on the hips of her stripy trousers. 'What is it?'

Keep calm, Jack — just act bored and she'll go home. He shrugged. 'What's it look like?'

'Dunno — never seen anything like it before. A rubbish skip on roller skates?'

'*A rubbish skip on roller skates?* Incredible — you wouldn't know a Jaguar from a jelly baby! Actually, it's a top of the range, fuel-injection, turbo-charged racing ca— Hey! What d'you think you're doing?'

Clang! She bashed the bonnet with a freckled fist, then down she knelt and squinted underneath, her pigtails pointing at half past twelve. 'So why's it got five wheels?'

What? Jack glanced at the undercarriage. *Zippity-flibbit — she's right.* 'For acceleration. It's a — er — five-wheel drive. It does 0 to 60 in three and a half seconds, cruising speed 500 miles an hour.'

'Oh.' She bent back an aerial and let it ping.

'Stop that, will you? That's the Sat Nav mast.'

'If you say so.'

Wrong! It was all going horribly wrong. He was supposed to keep The Fruitcake out and now she was strolling around as if she owned the place, humming to herself like a wasp at a picnic.

'Guess what?' she said, slapping the wall. 'My bedroom's just through there.'

That's all I need — Little Miss Big-Nose in snoring range. And what exactly was she up to now — striding towards the desk? Disaster times a thousand: *she's opening the book.*

'*This book belongs to Jack Dash.* Hey — that's you, isn't it?' She turned the page. 'And what are these splats supposed to be?'

Jack went cold: sandwiched in those pages, millimetres from her hand, his precious feather lay. He had to stay calm and he had to think fast. 'Put that down — it's modern art and it's very valuable!'

'*Valuable?*' She was peering at the bluebottle drawing the way his mum looked at road maps. 'Looks like it was done by a three year old. I'm really good at art. I won the Christmas Card Competition two years running and my teacher said . . .'

'Leaping lizards!' Jack was hopping from foot to foot and pointing to the window. 'What's that?'

'What?'

'Outside – on the chimney – looks like an otter.'

'Don't be daft.' But she put down the book and went over anyway, just to check. Perfect: she'd flung the window open and now she was poking her head out. 'Must've been a pigeon. Hey – I can see the pavement from here. Ooh, there's Mrs Tangent from number 28 – she's a right grump!' She was halfway out now, calling to Jack over her shoulder. 'Let's drop a water bomb on her head!'

Here's my chance – I'll hide the feather where that freckled nose won't find it. Step by tiny step, Jack inched towards the desk. He whisked the feather behind his back and tucked it into his waistband. *I have to get her out of here and fast.*

'Got any balloons?' said Coco, dropping back to the floor. 'Mrs Tangent's right under the . . .'

'Shh!' Jack leaned forward, cupping his ear. 'Your dad's calling.'

'Can't be – he's gone out.' She beamed at him. 'It's brilliant you've moved next door – we're going to have so much fun.'

'I meant your mum.' Jack grabbed Coco's wrist and tugged her to the door. 'I heard your mum calling and she sounded *furious*.'

'My mum lives in Spain.'

'Oh,' said Jack. 'I just remembered – it was *my* mum. That's it – I've got to go to the taxidermist. We're having our emu stuffed.'

'Your mum? I didn't hear anything.'

'She's got a very quiet voice – her larynx fell out when she was a baby.' Jack opened the door. 'You better go.'

'What are you on about? I just met your mum and she . . .'

Bam! Jack slammed the door and before she knew it, The Fruitcake was stuck on the landing.

The handle rattled. 'Jack?'

Phew, phew, triple phew. He leaned on the door with all his weight. *She didn't find the feather and now she'll go away.*

'Jack, it's important. You can't go out – not that like that.'

Go-away-go-away-go-away-go-away . . .

'**JACK!**' she yelled. 'You know that emu you were on about? One of its feathers is stuck to your bum.'

EIGHt

Coco McBean had left at last, but her nose was bigger than an aardvark's and she'd poked it all over the place. She'd found the car, she'd found the book and she'd even seen the feather. And if she found out what it could do? Jack shuddered. *Volcanic eruptions ... alien invasions ... dinosaurs roaming the streets!*

Time for drastic action – she could come back any moment and he had to keep her out. But how? . . . a booby trap? . . . a burglar alarm? . . . a guard dog? Bingo! A big, black dog with a bloodthirsty bark – *that* would send her pigtails skyward.

He yanked the feather from the waistband of his jeans. He opened the book at an empty page, sat down and stared at the paper. *Relax,* he thought, *and don't draw five legs.* He circled his hand to loosen his wrist and, one by one, he stretched out his fingers. 'Okey dokey,' he said, breathing deep. 'I'm ready.'

He drew a sausage for a body. *Not bad* . . . He added a head with a sloping snout and zigzags for the fangs . . . *not bad at all.* He drew paws . . . two eyes . . . a shiny, black nose – tick – tick – tick – *and mustn't forget the whiskers.* Then he tilted back his chair, clasped his hands behind his head and puffed out his cheeks. *If this doesn't sort The Fruitcake out, then I'll eat my* . . .

'ARF-ARF!'

Thundering trumpets – its bark was as loud as a car alarm! Had he left the bedroom door open? Jack ran to check, then turned around and froze – it was the weirdest-looking creature he'd ever seen: bigger than a bulldog and twice as fat. He gulped. Fourteen kilos of untamed rubber with added teeth was heaving itself over the floorboards towards him.

Great hairy gibbons – it's a sea lion! Keep calm, Jack. First sign of fear and it'll have your toes for jelly beans.

'D-down boy!'

The sea lion glared at him.

'G-girl!' he said. 'I mean girl. And that's a really pretty beard, by the way.'

What was she doing? She'd stopped beside his racing car and was snuffling round the bumper. Now she was looking in the side mirror. She cocked her head and fluttered her eyelashes. *Gggrrrr* – she hooked her lip into a snarl and a hairy face growled back at her. *Crunch* – she clamped her jaws around the mirror and with a twist of her head she tugged it.

'My racing car!' cried Jack, tears

pricking his eyes. 'My top of the range, fuel-injection, turbo-char—'

Clank!

He slid his hands over his face: he couldn't bear to look.

KERCHANG!

The mirror skidded across the floor. 'Stop vandalising my vehicle, you brute!'

RRR-I-PP!

And what was that? He peeped through his fingers: *No – please – no!* She was plunging her teeth into the passenger seat. *I gotta to do something.*

Like a gazelle on the plains of the Kalahari, he sprang – into the air, three metres or more, and – *boomph!* – on to the sea lion. Over he rolled, clinging to her belly by his half-chewed nails, leg over flipper, down and up and round and – *thud!* – on his chest she landed, heavy as a suitcase and grinning like a zip.

Jack sprawled on the floor, fighting for breath as her face loomed lower. Her hungry eyes glowed, saliva drooling from her whisker. He thrashed his head from side to side. He pushed and he heaved till his triceps trembled and he thought his lungs would burst. *Squished by an over-stuffed sea lion – what a way to go!* He clenched his eyes shut. *Goodbye bedroom . . . goodbye world . . . Goodbye magic feather.*

Tock, tock, tock – the seconds seemed to pass like hours, crowding his mind with the things he could have drawn: *a Creme egg as big as a football . . . an all-in-one games console popcorn machine . . . a twin-rotor helicopter with an ejector seat and a luminous nose and an inflatable trampoline suspended underneath.*

'I could have had them all . . .' *Boom-boom-boom* went his heart, flooding his veins with warrior blood. 'And I won't be stopped by a brainless ball of black blubber!

With a mighty thrust, Jack pushed the sea lion off his chest and rolled her on to the floor. He staggered to his feet, whipped off his scarf and looped it over her head.

'Gotcha!'

NINE

The sea lion gazed up at Jack, with eyes like melted chocolate and her flippers pinned to her sides.

'Don't give me that!' he wheezed. 'You wouldn't exist if it wasn't for me – and this is the thanks I get? A mangled car seat and a splintered rib cage?' He clutched at his heart, still banging in his chest. 'You're worse than The Fruitcake, you know that? You're a . . . a fur-brained, flipper-footed, dog-gone-wrong!'

She trembled. She tilted her head to one side. She tried to lift her flipper and then she let it drop.

'Oh no, you don't,' said Jack. 'You don't fool me with the soppy act. You've blown it, fuzz-face. I'm gonna drag you out when the coast's clear and dump you in the dustbin by the front . . . Huh?'

She dropped her head. A teardrop trickled down her snout. It slid off the end of her whisker and – plip! – it splashed to the floor.

'Please don't cry.' He knelt down beside her to untie the scarf. 'I . . . I won't dump you anywhere. I'll look after you, I promise.'

The sea lion blinked and raised her head a little.

Hold it right there – a pet sea lion? I must be leaking brain juice. He wiped a scrap of car seat off her whisker and tickled her under the chin. *Why not? I can hide her in my bedroom — Mum and Dad'll never know. I'll train her with treats like they do on the telly.* 'We'll go for a spin in The Ravioli Ultra,' he said. 'You can be my co-driver.'

Her eyes filled with amber light and she laid a velvet flipper on his knee.

'We'll be famous. *Jack Dash and his Secret Sea Lion — Formula One Sensations!* And you'll need a name . . . like Selina . . . or Sandra . . . or — or Sardina! *Sardina, the Supersonic Sea Lion.* It's perfect. It's brilliant. Give me a high five!'

Up she sat and slapped his palm with her flipper.

'Uh-oh . . .' Jack gaped at the puddle spreading across the floorboards. He wriggled his toes. 'My sock,' he cried. 'It's gone all sticky!'

'Arf!'

'No!' he said. 'Please . . . Tell me you didn't wee!'

'Arf-arf!'

'Things are gonna have to change, Sardina. Training camp starts here.' He peeled his steaming sock off and flung it into the corner. 'Now where's that feather?'

†EN

Hang on Sardina, we're taking the corner at breakneck speed. 0 to 60 in three and a half seconds — cruising speed 500 miles an hour. Brm-brrm-brrmm . . .

'Why's he growling like that?' Mr Dash put down his knife and fork and frowned at Jack. 'Eat your lunch properly.'

Jack sawed off a slice of sausage and stuck it in his mouth. *Chew, chomp — must act normal. Chew, chomp — must act normal.*

'Dumpling . . .' said Mum, with her fidgety face on. 'Are you sure you're all right?'

Jack slid the ketchup bottle over the

kitchen table. *Me and Sardina in my very own super-car — a lean, mean racing machine — brm-brrm-brr . . .*

'Dotty,' said Dad. 'This can't go on — the boy's out of control. I've got enough to worry about: I've had a letter. Special delivery.'

'A letter?'

'From the mayor,' said Dad, with his head in his hands.

'The mayor?' She let out a little squeak. 'Did you hear that, Jack? That's Dad's new boss.'

Brrmm-brrmm. 'Huh?'

'The most important man in the whole of Curtly Ambrose and he's written to your father! Well, go on then — tell us what he says.'

Dad fished the letter out of his pocket and handed it to Mum.

'*I'm delighted to welcome you to our lovely town,*' she read. 'Oh, how thoughtful! What a nice touch.'

'Keep reading,' said Dad.

'*Payment of the Welcome Tax is now due for the recent occupation of your residence . . .*' She looked at her husband. 'I don't understand.'

'It's a bill,' said Dad. 'He's taxing us for moving in.'

'Oh . . .' She looked at the letter again and chewed her bottom lip. 'And what are all those sums?'

'That's how much we have to pay. See? They multiply our house number by the total number of windows at the front and back of the property.'

'So that's thirty-three times – er . . .'

'It's a small fortune,' said Dad. 'And he's coming round in person to pick up the money.'

'In person . . . ? Oh – that's wonderful!' She closed her eyes and shivered. 'The Mayor of Curtly Ambrose is coming to visit us – here, in this house. Our very own home!' She clasped her hands together and sighed. 'When's he coming?'

'Tomorrow morning. Eleven o'clock.'

'Tomorrow morning? Oh Lionel, this is terrible . . . *terrible!* My hair's a mess and the house isn't ready and you still haven't polished the china cups. Dumpling . . .' She reached across the table and grasped Jack's hand.

Uh-oh. Eat up and get outta here quick.

'I want you on your best behaviour for the mayor. We've got to make a good impression. We're relying on you, sweetie. We want you to make us proud. We want you to . . . to . . .' She wrinkled up her nose. 'What's that?' She stood up and sniffed the air like a meerkat. 'Is it the rubbish bags?'

What's she on about now? Gotta get back to Sardina — she's all alone with The Ravioli Ultra and my drawings of the . . .

'Fish!' said Mum. 'That smell — it's definitely fish.' She wafted her hand in front of her face. 'And it's getting worse.'

Fish? Oh no, oh no, oh no – Sardina's treats.

'Good grief, you're right!' said Dad. He stood up and strode into the hall, clasping his handkerchief to his face. 'And it's even stronger out here.'

Right by Dad's foot, Jack could see a halibut flapping on the floor. And here came a conger eel slithering down the stairs. *Must act normal, must act normal.*

'It's dreadful,' said Mum. 'First bluebottles and now this horrid smell. Lionel, what are we going to do? How can I entertain the mayor tomorrow with fishy odours in the hall?'

Jack gulped. A starfish was stuck to the fridge and an octopus's tentacle was waving from the sink.

Chew, chomp – must act normal.

'I'll call the pest control people,' said Mr Dash, reaching inside his jacket for his phone. 'They can clean the whole house from top to bottom.'

Sausage sprayed across the table. *Top to bottom?* Jack pictured them opening his bedroom door and his tummy flipped like a pancake. 'Sardina!' he cried. 'The Ravioli Ul—'

'Sardine ravioli? Dumpling, what *are* you talking about?'

'Make him stop, Mum. It's cruel!' Jack leaped up and grabbed her by the sleeve.

'Don't be silly, sweetie – we can't have fishy smells and flies in the house.'

'Flies have feelings too, same as you and me.'

'Will you *stop* this nonsense?' said Dad, pulling an oyster out of his pocket. He frowned and scratched his head, then slipped it back inside his jacket and pulled out his phone. 'Ah – yes – hello – is that the Verminators? . . . I'd like to make an urgent appointment . . . first thing tomorrow morning? . . . Perfect . . . yes, yes – it's number 33, Quarantine Street.'

ELEVEN

Jack opened his bedroom door and his jaw dropped to his trainers: Sardina was sprawled on the bonnet of The Ravioli Ultra, her tummy as round as a planet. She looked at him with a grin, then spat out a fish head and burped.

Dead fish littered the floorboards – hundreds of them! Why had he drawn so many? Bones, tails, gizzards and gills . . . cat fish, dog fish, moon fish, frog fish, one fish finger, half a squid and, in the corner, another puddle of wee.

'Don't panic,' he told himself. 'Keep

calm. And hide them in the sleeping bag.'
He bent down and prodded a Sockeye
Salmon – yuck, yuck, triple yuck: it was
stiff, it was wet and it stank. 'Or under the
floorboards or . . . or – I know!' He dragged
a chair over to the window. 'I'll dump them
on the roof.' Up he climbed and pushed the
window open.

'COO-EEE!'

Snakes alive, it's Coco McBonkers! She
was leaning out
of her bedroom
window, waving
from behind a TV
aerial.

'You didn't tell
me you had a dog.'

'I don't.' The chair wobbled. Something was tickling his foot.

'You're hiding something – I know it.' She leaned forward. 'Why's your face twitching?'

Jack pressed his lips together and clenched his fists. Sardina was at his ankle again. '*Get off!*' he hissed, then popped his head back out. 'It isn't.'

'Arf!'

'What's that then?' said Coco.

'O u c h !'
First death by tickling – now she's gnawing my Achilles tendon.

His bottom lip trembled. 'It's n-nothing,' he said. *Hold it together, Jack.* He clutched the windowsill and gave his leg a shake.

'Arf–arf!'

'It's a dog – I heard it and it's in your bedroom. I love dogs!' Coco beamed at him. 'I'm coming round.'

'You can't.' Sardina's nose was up his trousers and she was licking his shin like a lolly.

'Why not? Your mum said I can come whenever I liked. She said you need friends.'

'She said *what?* Well, she's gone to bed.'

'I'll ask your dad then.'

'He's gone to bed as well.'

'But it's only half past three.'

Does she never give up? 'He's ill. He's got

Myxomatosis. In fact, he might be dying.'

'Mixy-your-wotsits?' Her face clouded for a moment, then split into a smile. 'I get it – you're joking. I nearly fell for that one. I'll bring my ball and we can go to the park and play fetch.'

'NO! I mean . . . we can't.'

'Why not? Come on – it'll be fun.'

'My dog – er – she doesn't have legs.'

'Doesn't have legs?' Coco twizzled her pigtail and looked at him sideways. 'That's the weirdest thing I ever heard – what kind of dog is she?'

'Um . . .' *Think, think, think.* 'She's a short-haired Sardine Terrier.'

'This I've *got* to see. I'll be there in three minutes.'

S'no good, I gotta tell her. Jack swallowed hard. *Here goes:* 'Actually she's a – er – sea lion.'

'What?'

'She's not a dog, she's a sea lion.'

'Yeah, right,' said Coco.

'I promise – I swear it. She's in my bedroom and she's out of control and she tried to eat my racing car and there's fish everywhere and I've got to hide it all by tomorrow morning before Mum and Dad find out.'

Coco leaned forward. *'Really?'*

'Really.'

'Cool!'

'What am I gonna do?' said Jack.

'Easy. Lower it out of the window.'

'I can't do that!' He looked down at Sardina and patted her flipper. 'She's very sensitive – and believe me, things get soggy when she's excited.'

'Not the *sea lion*, you dongle, the *car*. Look!' Coco was pointing at the kerb. 'There's a parking space.'

Jack craned his neck over the roof tiles at the street far below. 'O-*kaay* . . . and how do I lower a car out of my bedroom window exactly?'

'I'll get the high-pressure hose. Stay right there.'

'*What?*' he cried. 'No – wait!' Too late: she'd slammed her window shut. Hurricane Coco was coming round.

tWELVE

'Poo-eee!' Coco dumped the reel of hosepipe at Jack's feet and flapped her hand over her nose. 'It's whiffy in here. Smells like a . . . I don't believe it! A real, live *sea lion*!'

'ARF!' barked Sardina, waving her flipper.

'*Shhh!*' Jack bundled Coco through the door and clicked it shut. 'Keep your voice down. If my parents find out they'll sell me on eBay.' He looked at the hosepipe and swallowed. 'You're not gonna set that thing off again, are you?'

'Course not. D'you think I'm daft or something? We'll tie it to the car and reel it out through the window.'

'Hmm ...We could fix it to the bumper, I s'pose. I'm pretty good at knots.'

'Told you I'd sort it.' Coco beamed at him. 'So what's the sea lion's name?'

'Sardina,' said Jack.

Up Sardina sat and beamed at Coco. She slapped her flippers and burped up a fish head.

'Sardina Dash,' said Coco. 'Wow. Sounds like a film star. Does she do any tricks?'

'We don't have time for that – we gotta clear this room out before the Verminators arrive.'

'This is going to be the best fun ever.'

Coco shuffled off her backpack, plunged in her arm and pulled out a fluffy bath mat. 'You'll need this.'

Jack blinked. 'What is it?'

'It's a very cunning disguise.' She draped the mat over Sardina's back and grinned. 'See?'

'Nope. Don't get it. What's she s'posed to be?'

'A short-haired Sardine Terrier, obviously. No one will ever guess.' She reached into her backpack and plonked a bright red box on the floor. 'And you'll need this, too.'

'Salt?' said Jack. 'What do I need salt for?'

'Salt water, of course – it's a sea lion's

natural habitat. Ooh, look . . .' she said. 'My Sherbet Slammers!' She shook the paper bag in his face. 'There's one left. D'you want it?'

'You must think my brain's capsized – I wouldn't eat that thing if I was strapped to a yak and dragged up Everest backwards.'

'Please yourself.' She popped it into her mouth and rummaged around her backpack again. 'Now where did I put my ball? I'm sure I packed it.'

'You don't get it, do you? We're running out of time. Where are we gonna hide the fish? They're everywhere and they stink.'

'Simple,' she said, as she scrabbled through her backpack. 'Bung 'em in the boot of the car.'

The boot. Jack ran to the car and yanked it opened. *Hmmm . . . maybe that's not such a bad idea.* 'Hey, Coco – help me load them in, will you?'

'No way, José. I'm not touching them – they're gross.'

Jack sighed. 'Okay then, I'll do it myself.' He held his breath, scooped up an armful of fish from the floor and, with a shudder, he stuffed them inside.

In went another load. Another. And another.

'DUCK!'

Jack hit the

floor as a yellow ball shot past his shoulder.

Into the air Sardina dived and – **biff** – she bounced it back with her flipper.

'Wow,' said Coco. 'Nice backhand!' She thrust her arm into her backpack and pulled out a frying pan. 'Okay, sweet-cheeks – let's start a match.' Swing went the pan – **bong** went the ball – and – **biff!** 'Great shot, Sardina – love: fifteen.' **Bong** – **biff**. 'Fifteen all!'

'Stop doing that, will you? I need some help here.' Jack picked himself up, slammed the boot shut and wiped his hands on his jeans.

Bong – **biff**. 'Thirty: fifteen!'

'How exactly are we gonna lift the car out of the window?'

'We'll use a ramp.'

'A ramp?' said Jack. 'Silly me – now why didn't I think of that? I always keep a spare ramp in my bedroom just for emergencies.' *Crrr-ack!* 'What d'you think you're doing?'

'Perfect,' said Coco, clutching a dusty floorboard. 'Once you get your fingers under, they snap out nice and easy.'

'You – you've just ripped a hole in my bedroom floor.' *Crrr-ack!* 'I don't believe it – you've done it again!'

Coco laid the boards side by side on the floor beneath the window, then propped up their ends on the sill. 'One designer ramp,' she said. 'Genius!'

'It'll have to do, I s'pose ... But leave the tying-up bit to me, will you?' He grabbed one end of the hose and slipped it under the bumper. 'This bit takes skill.'

Through the car window he wiggled the hosepipe, looping it round the passenger seat, then he tied it with a Double Slippery Buntline Hitch Knot. 'Not bad. Not bad at all.' He rubbed his hands together and grinned. 'What d'you think, Coco?'

She laid the frying pan on the floor and rolled her eyes. 'I'm trying to serve, Jack. What d'you want?'

'I've tied the car up. It's time to lower it out.'

'Wait there, Sardina – I'll be back in a tick.'

'Arf–arf!'

'First things first,' said Jack. 'I'll hold on to the hosepipe while you push the car up the ramp. Then we'll nudge it through the window and lower it bit by bit.'

'Okey dokey. I'll give it a try.'

'Hmm . . .' said Jack. 'Or maybe we should use a pulley system to take some of the weight.' He strolled over to the door and scratched his head. 'If I wrap the hosepipe around the . . . *belching buzzards, what are you doing?*'

'Pushing the car up the ramp, like you said. It's actually not that heavy.'

Jack clutched on to the door handle to steady himself. Beside her on the windowsill perched The Ravioli Ultra, its bonnet thrust through the window frame, its bristling rear and hind wheels high in the air.

'Look what happens when I tap the boot,' she said. *Cree-ak* – down tipped the car boot into the room and up went the bonnet through the open window. Down-up, down-up – rocking on the sill like a seesaw. 'See?' she said. 'Perfectly balanced!'

Jack's mouth fell open. A whimper escaped from somewhere deep inside him. 'Okay, Coco – don't move – don't blink – don't even speak.' He tiptoed towards her, nozzle in hand. 'I want you to listen *very, very carefully*. See this?'

'M-hm,' she said, as he held it up to her face.

'This is the nozzle that's attached to the hosepipe that's attached to the car, okay?'

'M-hm.'

'I need to secure it or the car goes kaput – so I'm going to wind it round the door handle. Got it?'

'M-hm.'

'Then I'll wrap it round the desk.'

Coco nodded.

'And whatever you do, don't touch the car till I –'

'Whoopsie!'

The nozzle whipped out of Jack's hand. He lunged. 'Grab that hosepipe!' he yelled, as it shot across the floor like a snake.

'Arf-arf!' Sardina was clapping. Coco was giggling. And The Ravioli Ultra was gone.

Jack blinked. He opened his mouth and closed it again. 'Coco,' he croaked, his face as pale as a celery stick. 'What did you do to my car?'

'I think it overbalanced.'

'I told you!' he cried. 'Didn't I just tell you? I said: *don't move*. I said: *don't blink*. I said . . .'

'Stop knitting knickers, it'll be fine.'

'Fine?' Jack collapsed to the floor as his knees folded beneath him. '*Fine?* You just shoved my racing car out of the window!'

'I didn't *shove* it, exactly – I must've nodded my head by mistake.' She peered over the windowsill. 'That's weird – it's sort of floating in mid-air. Come and have a look.'

Jack stumbled to her side and leaned out of the window. 'That's incredible!' The Ravioli Ultra was hanging below them, swinging and twisting like an enormous pendulum. 'It's defying gravity. I didn't just draw a racing car – I drew a masterpiece of modern engineering.'

'No, you dim-bat – the hosepipe got caught. My dad's spray attachment is jammed under the window latch.'

'Oh,' said Jack. 'Right. Well, don't panic. I'll wiggle it free.'

'Bad idea. We've run out of hosepipe.'

He leaned out of the window again. *She's right* . . . The hosepipe wasn't long enough. It wouldn't reach the ground. The Jack Dash 700 Ravioli Ultra was stuck!

'So what do we do now, Wonder Woman?'

'No probs. My dad's got a box of decorations.'

'Decorations?'

'You know — fairy-lights and tinsel — we'll hang 'em off the aerials and disguise the car.'

'Christmas decorations in the middle of May? Great idea, Coco — one of your best! Tell me something: are you always this stupid or is today a special occasion?'

'Oooh, who twanged *your* elastic? I was only trying to help.'

'Well, don't bother. You're useless! You're an idiot! You're a freckle-faced, banana-brained, ketchup-coloured criminal!'

Coco blinked. 'Fine,' she said. 'I won't!' She dusted off her hands and stalked to the door. 'No wonder you haven't got any friends.'

'What are you doing? You can't go now!'

'Watch me.'

'But what do I do with the car?'

'How should I know?' she called over her shoulder. 'I'm a banana brain, remember?'

Thud. The door slammed, the wall shuddered and a yellow ball bounced once . . . twice . . . and dropped at Jack's feet. 'Arf-arf!' Sardina gazed up at him and slapped her flippers together.

It was going to be a long, long night.

tHIRtEEN

Where did it all go wrong? Nearly midnight and Jack hadn't slept a wink; beside him lay Sardina, her flipper wedged in his armpit. *This should've been the best day ever . . . I could've had it all. And then Coco came along with her stupid hosepipe.* He rolled on to his back. *Now my racing car's hanging out of my bedroom window and I'm sharing a sleeping bag with a sea lion.*

'Grrr-ruff-ruff . . . Grrr-ruff-ruff.' Her snores rumbled like distant thunder and her breath smelled worse than school fish pie. 'Grrr-ruff-ruff . . .' she batted her flipper and whacked him on the ear.

I've had it. He sat up and stared into the night. *I – I can't take any more.* Out he wriggled and stumbled through the dark.

Squitch!

Yeeuch! He flicked on the light and peeled a herring off his heel. And then he saw it: the box of salt. *Salt water . . . a sea lion's natural habitat. A-ha!* An idea lumbered into his aching mind. *It's risky . . .* He eased open his bedroom door and peered down the stairs, *but if I don't get some sleep, my head will crack and my eyes will pop and I'll be picking my teeth up off the floor.*

'Sardina!' he hissed. 'Wake up!'

'Grrr-ruff-snort!' She opened her eyes, shuffled out of the sleeping bag and waddled after him, into the half-light of the landing.

'Wait here,' he whispered. 'When I give the signal, follow me down to the bathroom. And whatever you do, don't make any noise. Got it?'

'ARF-ARF!'

'*Shh!*' He grasped her by the flipper and looked deep into her eyes. 'This is important – I'm relying on you. If you wake up Mum and Dad, it's goodbye Formula One and hello dustbin.'

Down the stairs Jack tiptoed, pausing outside the bathroom door, next to his parents' bedroom. Not a sound. He glanced up at the top step and dangled the half-squished herring in the air. Sardina's eyes widened. Would she? . . . Could she? *Yes!* Down the stairs she launched herself – headfirst and flippers splayed, like an aeroplane coming in to land. *Ka-dump!* She hit the bedroom door. Jack stiffened, heart thumping . . . Someone murmured . . . Silence again. He crept into the bathroom. *Grrr* . . . He turned around: Sardina was eyeing herself in the full-length mirror.

'Don't start that again!' He dropped the herring into the bath. 'In you get,' he whispered.

She glanced up at him, then peered over the rim, licked her lips and heaved herself over the side.

Now for the seawater. Jack turned on the cold tap and tipped in the salt, then sat on the side of the bath, shivering as he watched the water froth around her. He wrapped his arms around himself. *The best day of my life . . . and I'm sitting on a bath in the middle of the night, twenty-four-and-a-half miles from home.* He turned off the water and yawned. His eyes felt as heavy as his heart.

'Oh, Sardina . . .' He reached out to stroke her head. 'How'd we get into this mess?' She gazed up at him, her chin resting on the soap dish and her dark eyes shining through the gloom. 'Don't worry, I'll think of something – I'll get the Ravioli Ultra sorted,' he said. 'We're a team, you and me. We'll be on that race track before you can shake your tail flippers.'

In the shadows, he could see the gleam of her smile.

Jack hauled himself to his feet. He pinched his nostrils together and kissed her whiskery cheek. 'Good night,' he whispered.

Her dark shape stirred in the moonlight as he tiptoed to the door, then she sank into the water, silver bubbles rising to the surface.

FOURTEEN

Jack woke in a square of sunlight that stretched across his sleeping bag and over the dusty floorboards. He sat up and rubbed his eyes – what was that smell? He picked up the sock lying by his ear and sniffed it. *No worse than normal, so where's it coming from?* And then he remembered. Fish.

It was all coming back to him: Coco . . . the car . . . the ramp . . . the hosepipe . . . *Foaming flannels – Sardina's in the bath! I gotta get her out before Mum and Dad go in there.*

He wriggled out of his sleeping bag, yanked on his jeans, jammed on his trainers and careered down the stairs, *thump-thump-thump*, three at a time, into the bathroom, skidding across the tiles. Bang – his knees hit the side of the bath. Empty.

'Okay. No problem. She's probably hiding.' He wrenched open the cupboard and rummaged through the towels. Nothing. He peered round the door, into his parents' bedroom. Nobody. He checked under the bed, rifled through the wardrobe and tipped the laundry basket on to the floor. *Where is she? And where are Mum and Dad?* Down he raced, *thump-thump-thump*, stopping on the landing to check the loo.

Nope. She must be downstairs in the –

Cock-a-doodle doo! The doorbell. Jack peered over the banister railing down into the front hall: the kitchen door was opening. Footsteps.

'That'll be the Verminators,' Dad was saying. 'I'll let them in.'

Jack crouched in the shadows at the top of the stairs. Here came his father in a suit and tie, striding down the hall to the front door. So far, so good – he didn't look like a man who'd just had breakfast with a sea lion.

So if Mum's in the kitchen and Dad's in the hall . . . where's Sardina? She can't have just disappeared, he thought. *Or maybe she can . . . after all, she appeared out of nowhere, didn't she?* He gulped. *Would she really leave without saying goodbye?*

'Thank heavens you're here,' said Dad, as he opened the front door. 'We're expecting a visitor at – oh!'

'Hi, Mr D – how's your Mixy-your-wotsits?'

'Coco! It's – er – not a very good time at the . . .'

'S'okay, I know the way.' She ducked under Dad's arm and scampered up the stairs. 'Jack, you weirdo – why are you sitting on the landing in the dark?' She giggled. 'And what's with the jeans and pyjama combo?'

'Shh!'

She pulled up a pigtail. 'You what?'

'Get down,' Jack hissed. 'They don't know I'm up here.'

'About the car . . .' she whispered, crouching down beside him. 'Sorry I push—'

'The Ravioli Ultra!' He clapped his hand to his forehead. 'I forgot all about it.'

'I'll help you get it down and this time I promise I'll be careful.'

'We don't have time – Sardina's missing.'

'Sardina! Missing? When? How?'

'I dunno! She just went! We have to *do* something, Coco. What if she's in trouble? What if she's trapped somewhere and she can't get out?'

'Did you check the garden?'

'What for? She can't open the door.'

'Maybe someone left it open. We'll

sneak out the back while your mum and dad are busy and . . .'

Cock-a-doodle doo! Jack peered through the railings: Dad was opening the door again. 'Oh no,' he whispered. 'Oh no, oh no, oh no – the Verminators.' On the doorstep, he could see a tiny man in a white coat and a pointy beard. 'He'll tell Dad about the car and then we're for it.'

Coco squinted over the banister. 'I don't think he's noticed.'

'*Don't think he's noticed?* It's a top of the range, turbo-charged racing car – and it's dangling from a hosepipe right over his head!

'He wouldn't notice if it was dangling over his nostrils. Look.'

Outside the front door, the tiny man was struggling with the rose bush. 'Unhand me, you rascal!' he squeaked.

'Er, hello . . .' said Dad.

'Ah, there you are Madam,' said the man, wrenching his arm free. 'Most extraordinary behaviour . . . complete stranger . . . tried to grab me!'

Dad looked at the rosebush and back at the man. 'And you are . . . ?'

'Professor Scratchett.' He thrust out his hand and gazed up at Dad's ear. 'Of Itch and Scratchett, Pest Control Specialists and Verminators to the Queen. Experts in the removal of rats, fleas, weevils and cockroaches, bedbugs, silver fish, maggots and lice – to name but eight.'

'Come in,' said Mr Dash. 'There's no time to lose.'

'One moment please,' said the professor, fumbling in his top pocket. 'I'm a little short-sighted without these miraculous contraptions.' And he popped a pair of thick, square glasses on to his nose. 'A-ha! I can see the problem already.' He bent to pluck an insect from the doormat, held it aloft and sighed. '*Calliphora Vomitoria*.'

'Excuse me?'

'Otherwise known as the Common Bluebottle – a beauty of a specimen. Test-tube, please!'

'Good Lord!' Mr Dash staggered back as the hallway darkened: an enormous man was easing himself through the door, the buttons of his white coat straining across his chest. With fingers the size of jumbo hot-dogs he held out a tiny glass container into which Professor Scratchett dropped the dead bluebottle.

'Allow me to introduce my colleague, Itch,' said the professor, dusting off his hands.

'Good morning,' said Dad.

'Uh-oh,' said Jack. 'Here we go.'

But the enormous man just grunted.

Mr Dash paused. 'So, about this smell . . . Can you get rid of it?'

'Most interesting . . .' Professor Scratchett tipped back his head and sniffed. 'Aquatic, with hints of whiskered mammal. Yes, I think it can be successfully eradicated. Righty-ho – we'll begin on the ground floor and work our way upstairs. Itch, fetch the device from the van!'

The hall shuddered with his departing footsteps: *pah-doom, pah-doom, pah-doom* – and *slam* went the door behind him. A moment later and – *cock-a-doodle doo!* Dad opened the door again. Itch was cradling a large, rusting box in his arms.

'What on earth is that?' said Dad, as Itch placed it gently on the doormat.

'That, my good sir . . .' said Professor Scratchett, twirling his bowtie, '. . . is a masterpiece of modern engineering – the fumigation cannon.' He gave a little skip. 'Ta-dah!'

'*Fumigation cannon?* You're not going to fire it in here, are you? I'm expecting a very important visitor.'

'But of course − it's our most effective weapon in the war against biological aromas! This barrel,' he said, pointing to a tube at the front, 'extends like a telescope to a maximum of seven feet − approximately two point one three metres.' He opened a lid in the top and rubbed his hands together. 'And these are the aeration missiles.'

'Missiles?' Mr Dash peered inside.

'With which to bombard the contaminated area. But first, we must light the fuse. Matches, please, Itch!'

Pah-doom, pah-doom, pah-doom.

'Wait,' said Dad. 'There's no need to shut the −'

Slam!

Cock-a-doodle doo! Mr Dash sighed and opened the door again. Itch stepped inside with a tiny box of matches in his sausage fingers.

'Position the cannon, Itch,' Professor Scratchett cried. 'I'll fire her up!'

Coco jumped up and started up the stairs. 'They're aiming straight at us. Let's get out of here!'

'But what about Sardina? I promised I'd look after her.'

'Hey, Jack!' He could hear Coco calling from his parents' bedroom. 'Come and look at this.'

He buried his face in his hands. *Sardina's all alone somewhere . . . Alone. Abandoned. Trapped.*

'Birds,' called Coco. 'Ginormous white ones – and they're dive-bombing your car.'

If anything happens to Sardina, I'll never, ever forgive myself.

'Jack dumb-bum Dash – get a move on, before they . . .'

FIFTEEN

Coco stumbled out of Mrs and Mrs Dash's bedroom, down the stairs and on to the landing. Somewhere in the thick green smoke below, Professor Scratchett was clapping.

'J–Jack?' she spluttered. 'Get off the floor!' She knelt beside him and shook him by the shoulder. 'Come on – stop messing about.' She jabbed him in the ribs with her forefinger.

Slowly, very slowly, he opened his eyes. 'Ow,' he croaked. 'What d'you poke me for?'

'Cos you're a total clot-brain, that's why. What's the matter with you? Why didn't you get out of the way?'

'I – I dunno. My mind went all scrambled – the Sardinators . . . Vermdina . . . And I think I've ruptured my spleen.' He stood up and rubbed his hip. 'So what happened?'

'Oh, not a lot, just the usual: someone fired a cannon up the stairs.' She waved a tendril of smoke away with her hand and giggled. 'You should see yourself – your hair's gone green and it's sticking up like a pineapple top. And another thing – I reckon your . . .'

KER-RUMPH! The wall shook. The staircase shuddered.

'Like I was saying . . .' said Coco, 'your car.'

'My car? What about my car?'

'It's not my fault, okay? It was bouncing all over the place when the cannon went off – the birds were going crazy.' She shrugged. 'I knew that hosepipe wouldn't hold.'

'No,' Jack moaned. 'No, please, no.' He staggered to the banister and gripped the rail. Professor Scratchett was climbing the stairs.

'Mission accomplished,' said the professor, emerging through the smog. 'Stand aside, you two – it's time to tackle the lavatory!' *Thump. Thump. Thump.* And here came Itch, with the cannon in his arms and a snorkel clamped to his face.

Cock-a-doodle doo! Jack peered over into the front hall.

'Not again!' said Mr Dash. Clasping his handkerchief to his nose, he blundered through the haze. He fumbled for the handle and flung the front door open, gulping for air like a drowning man.

'Mr Lionel Dash?'

'Wh-what?' The green smoke was curling around him like seaweed as he peered into the daylight. He coughed. He spluttered. He bent over double and – **pheefff!** – he wheezed like a bagpipe.

'Lionel? What's going on?' Mrs Dash came scurrying to the door in her orange nightie and her lilac tiara. 'Is it *him*?'

The smoke cleared and a pair of shiny pointed shoes stepped on to the doormat, followed by a briefcase and a shiny head.

'Indeed it is I . . .' said the owner of the head, thrusting out a hairy hand. 'Donald Gristle, Mayor of Curtly Ambrose.'

SIXTEEN

'Wow,' said Coco, from the landing above. 'Is that really the mayor?'

Jack peered over the banister rail: his head was sweating like a lump of old cheddar. Black hair sprouted from his ears and his moustache drooped to his jowls. Gold rings sparkled on his fat hairy fingers and a chain of office gleamed around his bulging neck.

'Oh no,' he groaned. 'What's Mum doing now?'

'Your Majesty!' said Mrs Dash, sweeping the floor with a curtsey. 'We weren't expecting you for another hour. We're in a teensy bit of a muddle, I'm afraid.'

'Please, Madam. Just call me Mayor Gristle.'

'Would you like a hanky, Mayor Drizzle?' said Mum, fishing one out of her pocket. 'You've got wet paint all over your lovely jacket.'

'Not *paint*,' he said, his cheek twitching. 'Droppings.'

'Oh dear – did you have an accident?'

'Seagull droppings.' The mayor shuddered. 'There's a flock of them on your doorstep.'

'Excuse me?'

'*Birds*, Mrs Dash. Big, white, flappy things with beaks.'

'On our doorstep?' Mum craned her neck over the mayor's shoulder and gawped into the street. 'Goodness me,' she squawked. 'You're right!'

'I can't apologise enough,' said Dad. 'I don't understand what they're doing here.'

'They're nesting,' said the mayor, 'in the vehicle that is illegally parked on the pavement outside your house.'

Jack and Coco looked at one another.

'Vehicle?' said Dad. 'On the pavement?'

Jack's parents peered out on to the street.

'Golly!' said Mum. 'Is that really a *vehicle*? It looks more like a runaway fridge. We've never seen it before, have we Lionel?'

'Never,' said Dad. 'It certainly wasn't there yesterday.'

'Snivell!' the mayor bawled into the street. 'Bring the evidence!'

A car door slammed and a man in a suit and cap appeared at the door with a briefcase. Mayor Gristle clicked it open and retrieved a fish in a plastic bag.

'Perhaps you recognise *this*?' He dangled it before him like a poop-scoop sack. Froth appeared at the corners of his mouth.

'No,' said Dad, peering over his glasses. 'I don't recognise it at all.'

'Don't play the innocent with me, Mr Dash – it's a dead mackerel and you know it. There are two hundred and thirty-seven assorted fish concealed in the boot of the aforementioned vehicle, *weeks* past their sell-by date.' He returned it to his briefcase with a pat. 'I shall be sending this specimen to the DRC'

'DRC?'

'Department of Rotting Comestibles. This mackerel is a public menace and a threat to human health.' He licked the spittle from the corners of his mouth. 'This is serious – very, very serious. I'll have to fine you, I'm afraid.'

'Fine me?' Mr Dash went pale. 'What for?'

'Harbouring unsavoury foodstuffs. And there'll be another fine for the vehicle.'

Dad blinked. 'But . . .'

'It's parked on the pavement outside your property and that makes you responsible.' The mayor shook his head.

'No permit . . . no number plate . . . Dear me, that'll be pricey! Lock my briefcase in the car, Snivell – and don't let it out of your sight!' He thrust out his fat hand to Jack's parents. 'You can pay me in cash. Now.'

Dad patted his pockets and swallowed.

'Lionel?' said Mum. 'Why don't you nip down to the bank while I make us all a nice cup of tea? The kitchen's this way Mayor Fossil,' she said, as she ushered him into the hall.

SEVENTEEN

'Here's our chance,' said Coco, nudging Jack down the stairs. 'You keep the grown-ups talking while I check the garden for Sardina.'

'Are you out of your ginger mind? What am I s'posed to say, exactly?'

'Just keep smiling and look him the eye. Shame we don't have any chocolates,' she said. 'Mayors love chocolate.'

Chocolate . . . thought Jack, and his brain began to buzz. *Chocolate. Mayors. Mayors. Chocolate.* He could draw a whole box this time – with crinkly paper and a shiny bow

– and rows of fancy chocolates inside it. 'Coco,' he said. 'Stay right here – I'll be back in a minute!' And – *thump-thump-thump* – he pounded up the stairs.

Back he came – *thump-thump-thump* – three at a time, with a big, shiny box in his hands.

'Wowza!' said Coco. 'The mayor's going to love them.' She opened the kitchen door a crack: Mayor Gristle was sitting at the table and Mrs Dash was pouring the tea.

'You seem to have finished all the biscuits, Mayor Guzzle,' Mum was saying. 'Shall I open some more?'

'Won't say no to another packet,' he said, wiping his mouth with the back of his hand. 'And a slice of cake, if you've got one.'

'I'll go out the back,' Coco whispered. 'Make sure they don't see me, okay?'

'B–but . . .'

'Good luck,' she said and shoved him through the door.

'Dumpling? Come and . . .' Mum looked her son up and down as he staggered into the kitchen, from the pyjamas poking out at his ankles to his shock of green hair. She gave out a whimper. The teapot rattled in her hand.

'So this is young Master Dash . . .' said the mayor. 'What an extraordinary looking creature.'

Keep smiling . . . Look him in the eye . . .

'Jack,' said his mother, 'it's very rude to stare.'

What's Coco doing? Just over the mayor's shoulder, Jack could see her in the garden, jumping and shouting and flapping her hands. *She looks like she's dancing.*

'Come along, Dumpling – where are your manners?'

Coco's going loopy out there. She was pointing into the kitchen now, with a jab-jab-jab of her finger.

'I do apologise, Mayor Nibble. I don't know what's got into him today.'

But the mayor was looking at the box in Jack's hands. 'Are they chocolates?' he said. 'I never say no to a –'

BOOM! The kitchen walls shuddered. Mayor Gristle's teacup jumped off its saucer. 'What was that?' he spluttered.

'Nothing to worry about!' said Mum, dabbing the tea off his tie. 'Just a stranger playing football in the garden, I expect.'

'Playing football? Without a permit? Dear-oh-dear.' Mayor Gristle hauled himself to his feet. 'I shall have to investigate this.'

No, no, no — don't look in the garden. Jack ran round the table to block his way and thrust the chocolate box under his nose.

Mayor Gristle licked his lips. 'Don't mind if I do . . .' He tugged at the bow, opened the lid and twirled a hairy finger. 'Eeny, meeny, miney —'

BOOM!

'That's it,' said the mayor. 'I've had enough!'

'No!' Jack cried. Out in the garden Coco was doing an elaborate mime. 'I did it!'

'I beg your pardon?' said the mayor.

Keep smiling . . . Look him in the eye . . . Jack gazed up at the mayor and grinned, green smoke curling around his leg. 'That noise . . .' he said. 'It wasn't in the garden – it was me.'

'*You?*' The piggy eyes widened. He waved at the smoke with a hairy hand. 'What's the matter with you, boy?'

'Swamp fever,' said Jack. 'Had it for years. Makes my breakfast go funny.'

'Well, keep away from my chocolates, will you?' Mayor Gristle snatched the box from him and cradled it in his arms. He plucked one out and raised it to his parted lips.

'That's unusual,' said Mum. 'It's got feelers.'

The chocolate wriggled, wafting two little horns at the mayor.

Uh-oh, thought Jack. *That's no chocolate . . .*

The mayor peered at it and then down at the box: eleven snails were on the move, crawling from their paper nests. He dropped the box and staggered back, grabbed the edge of the kitchen table and sat down with a thud.

His face froze.

'Are you all right?' said Mum. 'Don't you like French chocolates?'

'**AAAAAAAAAARGGH!**' Up leapt the mayor, grasping the seat of his trousers. 'I've been ambushed . . . savaged . . . eaten alive! My rear end! My bottom! My poor, poor gluteus maximus!'

'Jack,' she cried. *'Do* something!'

'Um . . .' Jack scratched his head.

'Look at that . . . that *thing*!' The mayor pointed at a whiskery head poking from under the chair. 'That *monster* just bit me!'

Please, thought Jack, *tell me I'm dreaming.*

'Walrus!' roared the mayor. 'It's a blinking walrus!'

'ARF! ARF!'

This isn't a dream − it's a nightmare. Jack slumped to his knees. *Oh Sardina, what have you done?*

EIGHTEEN

'Don't panic,' wailed Mum. 'I'll put a plaster on it.'

'A *plaster*? I need surgery – I need a double buttock transplant!' screamed the mayor.

'The first-aid box! Jack – in the bathroom cabinet – get the first-aid box!'

Oh no. Jack flew out of the kitchen and up the stairs. *Oh no, oh no, oh no.* He grabbed the box from the bathroom cabinet, ran back down again – *thump-thump-thump* – and crashed into Coco in the hall.

'Jack!'

'Coco! Did you see what –'

'Arf–arf–arf!'

'Uh-oh.' They both poked their heads round the kitchen door.

'Just keep calm, Mayor Whistle – and try to think. Did you have a walrus with you when you left the office this morning?'

'Are you out of your tiny mind, woman? I've never seen the wretched creature before!' The piggy eyes narrowed. 'It's that son of yours, isn't it? He planted the walrus under the table!'

'Oh no,' said Mrs Dash. 'You don't plant walruses – you grow them in the sea.'

He pointed wildly at the kitchen door. 'It's that boy, I tell you – he's not normal.'

'Arf–arf!'

The mayor whirled round and glared at Sardina. 'That walrus is laughing at me!'

'Really?' said Mum. 'Are you sure?'

'Of course I'm sure – it cackled. Right at me – like this.' The mayor cocked an eyebrow and bared his yellow teeth.

'Arf-arf-arf!'

'Look!' he shrieked. 'It did it again.' Foam began to bubble at the corners of his mouth. He leaned into Sardina's face. 'So you think it's funny, do you?'

'Arf!'

'That does it,' he hissed. 'You're coming with me.'

Mayor Gristle strode into the hall, his eyes ablaze and the seat of his trousers torn to shreds. He flung the front door open.

'Snivell!' he bawled. 'Take the accused to my car!'

Out jumped the driver and hurried into the house, as Jack and Coco scurried back up to the landing.

'Hello?' said Dad, arriving on the doorstep, clutching his wallet. 'Is everything all right?'

'No!' barked the mayor. 'Everything is not all right. I'm confiscating your walrus.'

Dad blinked twice. He took off his glasses and wiped them on his sleeve: here came Snivell, staggering down the hall, swaying with the weight of Sardina in his arms.

'Strap it in the front seat and tape up its muzzle,' said the mayor. 'And come back pronto! I want you to document the crime scene and then you can phone the press.'

'Oh Lionel!' Mrs Dash came running down the hall. 'Thank goodness you're back! There's been an accident – call the nearest walrus sanctuary!'

'*Walrus sanctuary?*' Mayor Gristle turned to face her. 'Oh no, Mrs Dash,' he breathed. 'This beast is not on holiday. It's a criminal and criminals need to be punished.' He twirled his moustache and smiled. 'It's going to the DEAD unit.'

'DEAD Unit?' said Mum, clutching Dad's arm.

'Dangerous and Exotic Animal Disposal.'

On the landing above, Coco and Jack

stared at one other. *Bang!* The car door slammed and Snivell returned with his camera.

'I want fingerprints! Photographs from every angle!' Mayor Gristle glanced at his watch. 'I've got a meeting at eleven-thirty – Snivell, you have four minutes to gather the evidence. I'm going inside for a packet of biscuits.'

NINETEEN

Coco stood up. 'We've got to let her out.'

'Then what?' said Jack. 'It's three grown-ups against us.'

'We'll run for it.'

'But Sardina doesn't have any legs, remember?' He bashed his head with his fist – *think, think, think. I could draw a crane or an ambulance or . . . or . . .* 'I know!' he said. 'The Ravioli Ultra!'

'You what?'

'The racing car – I'll use it for the getaway.'

'You reckon it will work?'

'It takes more than a bump to stop The Jack Dash 700 Ravioli Ultra – it does 0 to 60 in three and a half seconds and it's right outside the front door. The mayor won't stand a chance.'

'But you don't have a licence.'

'Don't need one,' said Jack. 'Not for off-roading – I'll drive it on the pavement.'

Coco grabbed him by the elbow. 'I'm coming too.'

'You sure you can handle it?'

She nodded.

'We've got two minutes exactly.' He set the timer on his watch. 'Okay, Coco – here's the plan . . .'

Thump-thump-thump – Jack flew past the bathroom – *thump-thump-thump* – past Itch coming down the stairs with a piece of furniture – *thump-thump-thump* – and flung open his bedroom door.

'Is this your room, young man?' said Professor Scratchett, with a clothes peg on his nose. 'It contains some very interesting specimens!'

'Have you seen my racing gear? It's an emergency.'

'What happened here? Did your fish tank implode?'

One minute, forty-six seconds.

Jack grabbed his goggles from the box on the floor and jammed on his Viking helmet. He pulled off his pyjama top and wriggled into his t-shirt. *My gloves? Where are my . . .* 'Hang on, where was he going?'

'Who?' said the professor, rubbing his palms together.

'Your friend.' said Jack. 'Mr Itch. Where's he taking it?'

'What?'

'My desk,' Jack squawked. 'He was walking down the stairs with my desk on his shoulder!'

'He's taking it to the laboratory. It can't stay here – it's infested with *Anobium Punctatum.*'

'You what?'

'Furniture Beetle – commonly known as woodworm.'

'B–but it's got a feather in it!'

'Marvellous!' Professor Scratchett clapped his hands. 'We'll submit it for analysis.'

'You don't understand – I need it. I – I… Come back!' Jack snatched up his gloves off the floor and blundered out of the room.

One minute, seven seconds.

'You made it!' cried Coco, as he hurtled through the front door and into the sunlight.

'Arf-arf!' Sardina was sitting beside her, clapping her flippers. Seagulls were circling above The Ravioli Ultra, hovering and swooping and screeching.

'Where'd he go?' said Jack, looking this way and that.

'Who?'

'The big guy – Itch – the man with my desk. Where is he?'

'Who cares? I've got Sardina – the car's okay – let's get out of here. Where are you going?' she cried, as he pushed past her and sprinted up the pavement. 'Jack – come back – there isn't time!'

But he was running up the hill, his eyes as round as tunnels and his hair wild with panic. He skidded to a halt outside number 57, then he spun on his heel and sprinted back again.

'Jack, don't go weird on me now – it's just a mouldy, old desk and *we've got to leave!*'

'It's a catastrophe,' he wailed. 'It's worse than flash floods and black holes and . . .

and . . . That's him!' He shook her by the arm and pointed across the street to a truck on the corner of Vaccine Lane. *Brmm, brmm, brmm* — its engine was revving.

Jack checked his watch: *sixteen seconds and counting.* 'I'm going after him.' He yanked the door of The Ravioli Ultra open and leapt inside.

'Arf–arf!'

Sardina! Her snout was squished against the window. *I can't leave her here.* He closed his eyes. *And I can't take her with me — they'll submit her for analysis.* He could hear the seagulls calling. *I have to choose: it's the feather or Sardina.*

'You okay?' said Coco. 'You've gone all blotchy.'

Anything . . . I could have anything I want

. . . all I have to do is draw it and it's mine. He swallowed. *The feather . . . or Sardina.* He breathed in deep. *Goodbye Creme egg. Goodbye games console. Goodbye twin-rotor helicopter.* He opened his eyes and pushed the passenger door open. 'Come on, Coco – we've got a sea lion to save.'

tWENtY

Jack tightened the strap of his Viking helmet, tugged on his gloves and flipped his swimming goggles over his eyes. This was it, the moment he'd been waiting for: his very first race and he couldn't afford to lose it. He turned to Coco in the passenger seat, her head squished sideways under the roof and Sardina squashed on to her knees.

'Fasten your seat belts, this is gonna be hairy.' He grasped the steering wheel and sucked the air into his lungs. *Time to burn rubber.*

'There aren't any.'

'Huh?'

'There aren't any seatbelts,' said Coco. 'And there's no ignition either.'

'Huh?'

'The ignition, you odd-sock! You know, the bit where you put the key?'

He scanned the buttons and switches and dials on the dashboard – it had more controls than a cockpit. Why had he drawn so many? He twizzled his finger and pushed a button. 'This . . .' he declared, 'is the starter.'

BEEEEEEP!

'Pickle my aunt – it's the horn!' He flicked a switch. 'I meant this one – this is it.' A pair of wipers swept across the windscreen. He bit his lip and turned a knob. *Clunk.* Seagulls scattered into the sky as the roof flipped back.

'Jack ...' said Coco, narrowing her eyes, 'you do know how to work this thing, don't you?'

'Course I do – I just need to check the engine.' Out he sprang and yanked the bonnet open. There was no engine. *I must be one clown short of a circus – what kind of dumb-bell forgets to draw an engine?* This was a disaster. Disaster times what? There'd been so many he'd lost count. *No feather, no engine and, any second now, the front door's going to open and ... and ...* He could hear Coco calling his name. He looked at Sardina, gazing at him with her flippers on the bonnet and he turned away. *It's all my fault. They were counting on me and . . .*

'Coco McBean calling Jack Dash – come in please!'

How am I gonna tell her? He took a deep breath. 'Coco . . .'

She was waving and pointing inside the car. 'I've found something,' she yelled. 'Down here!'

'Coco, listen – about the engine . . .'

Her head disappeared beneath the dashboard. 'They look like pedals.'

Pedals? His drawing of the racing car flashed through his mind. *Pedals . . . that's right – on the floor, under the steering wheel – of course.* Jack leaped back into the driving seat and laughed out loud.

'What's the joke?'

'This . . .' he said, 'is no ordinary car: it's a fuel-free, environmentally friendly, foot-powered pedal car!' He readjusted his goggles and tweaked the rear-view mirror: the door of his house was opening; out stepped Snivell, swinging his car keys round his finger. *Uh-oh!* He was looking through his car window and shaking his head. Jack rammed his foot down and The Jack Dash 700 Ravioli Ultra rattled into action. *And we're off! Brm, brrmm, brrrmm.* Legs pumping like pistons – up-down, up-down – it zigzagged along the pavement.

'Wake me up when we reach the post box,' said Coco.

'Huh?'

'Can't you go any faster? We've only gone three metres.'

Jack checked the mirror and shuddered: Mayor Gristle was narrowing his piggy eyes and squinting in their direction, his face as red as a radish. 'Coco, I think he's seen us. If I can just make it to the next tree, it's downhill all the way.' His legs were pumping, his blood was thumping and every muscle throbbed. He squeezed his eyes shut and forced his feet to the floor. *Up-down — I can do it, up-down — I can do it.*

Clunk. The sound of a car door. Jack checked the mirror again. The mayor's car was pulling out into the road.

The pavement tilted, the pain eased and The Ravioli Ultra began to roll. *Up-*

down — I can do it. Up-down, up-down — now the pedals were turning themselves. The steering wheel shuddered. Houses, trees and lampposts flashed by; a seagull swooped; the wind whipped his hair over his eyes. 'I can't see a thing,' Jack yelled. 'Where is he?'

'Who?'

'Mayor Gristle, you fruitcake — where is he?'

'Dunno,' said Coco, swivelling round. 'Sardina's flipper's in the way.' She knelt up on the car seat and giggled. 'Ooh, he's right behind us and he doesn't look very happy.'

Mother of all maniacs — she was leaning over the boot and giving him the loser sign.

'Coco, has your brain backfired? He'll tear off your arm and beat you with the soggy end.'

'Not if we lose him first – hang a left here!'

Jack yanked the steering wheel and up tipped the pavement as they screeched around the corner on two wheels. 'Hold on to Sardina,' he yelled. 'We're in over-steer!'

Slam! They bounced to the ground and the main road hurtled into view.

'Slow down,' said Coco. 'That's the High Street.'

Hmm . . . now where did I draw the brakes?

'Jack, there's a lorry – SLOW DOWN!'

BEEP-BEEEP! Jack closed his eyes as they veered off the kerb and the clash of metal echoed through his skull.

tWENtY-oNE

'You all right?' Coco grabbed Jack by the sleeve and hauled him to his feet. A headlight crunched underfoot as he staggered out of the wreckage. Still clutching the steering wheel, he blinked at the remains of The Ravioli Ultra scattered over the tarmac. Sardina was gnawing the rear view mirror; a seagull flapped away with an aerial in its beak; a tyre freewheeled across the road and came spinning to a halt at the kerb. His dream was over.

'Asbo's!' cried Coco.

'What?'

'Asbo's supermarket – it's right across the street.'

'Lemme get this straight,' said Jack, sliding his goggles on to his forehead. 'We've just crashed a car with a runaway sea lion and we're being chased by a mayor who foams at the mouth – and you want to go shopping?'

'It's our only hope, you ding-dong – we've got to hide and we've got to hide fast. Now *come on*!'

With legs like jelly and Sardina lolloping at his side, Jack stumbled after her, over the road and through the car park.

'You'll have to help me lift her,' said Coco, wrenching a trolley from the bay. 'She weighs a ton and a half.'

'Coco, I'm not sure about this.'

'Relax,' she said, flipping back the baby seat. 'You're more uptight than a month-old sock.'

Through the sliding doors they went and into the bright lights of the shop. Shoppers leaped aside as they swept down the Fruit & Veg Aisle, swung round the confectionery pyramid and into Ready Meals. *Crash!* – a man in jogging shorts dropped his basket.

'Take off that helmet,' Coco hissed, as she swerved round a soup can rolling across the tiles. 'And lose the steering wheel. Everybody's staring.'

'Staring? Of course they're staring! Maybe you haven't noticed, but we're walking round a supermarket with a sea lion in our shopping trolley. Coco . . . are you even listening to me?'

She was peering into the chill cabinet: 'Ham and pineapple or cheesy chunks?'

'Stop talking pizza toppings. What are we gonna do?'

'Sardina's starving,' she said, squeezing her flipper. 'Let's have a picnic and then we'll take her home.'

'Arf!'

'*Home?*' said Jack. 'Mum and Dad'll hit the ceiling.'

'I didn't mean your house, numb-bum – I meant the zoo.'

'The zoo?'

'Well, that's where she's from . . .' She turned to look at Jack. 'Isn't it?'

'Coco . . .' Jack looked left and right, then lowered his voice, '. . . can you keep a secret?'

She nodded.

'Sardina doesn't come from the zoo. I – er – I . . .' He fiddled with a pizza box. *Have I lost my lid? This is The Fruitcake, remember? The one who toasted my tonsils and crumpled my car.*

'What?' said Coco. 'What did you do? Where's she from?'

'Doesn't matter.'

'Yes, it does. C'mon Jack, tell me – I'm your friend, remember?'

'You're *my friend?*' Jack put down the pizza box and looked her in the eye. 'Okay then – I drew her. I drew a picture of a sea lion and then it came to life.'

'Yeah, right – and your mum's got no larynx and your dad's got Mixy-your-wotsits.'

'I did, I swear it. I drew the car as well – and the fish. How d'you think they got into my bedroom?'

'Don't ask me – you're the one who's weird.' She reached into the chill cabinet and grabbed a tub of coleslaw. 'Is 500 grams extra creamy all right by you?'

'Coco, listen to me – I found a fea—'

'DUCK!' she yelled, as she ripped off the lid with her teeth.

What was she doing? *Oh no, oh no, oh no, oh no.* She was drawing back her arm like she was in a slow motion replay. *She's lost it. She's finally left her launch pad and gone into orbit.* Jack sank to his knees as the tub of coleslaw whistled past his ear.

'That's it!' He sprang to his feet and seized the trolley. 'I've had it with you and your stupid games. Me and Sardina are getting out of here.'

'No!'

'Forget it – I'm not hanging round while you get us all arrested.'

'*Wait!*'

She could beg all she liked, but it was too late. 'You're not my friend. You're unscrewed . . . you're unsafe . . . you're so far gone you've run out of rocket fuel!'

'Stop!' she yelled, but he swung the trolley round and headed for the checkout.

'JAA—'

Disaster to end all disasters: the Mayor of Curtly Ambrose was lurching up the aisle like a zombie, coleslaw dripping from his face, slashing the air with his arms. 'Walrus snatchers!' he spluttered. 'Hand it over this instant!'

Sardina whimpered, her whiskers quivering.

'Never!' yelled Jack. He swung the trolley round again and back up the aisle he ran – *ratter-clat-clat* – past the pizzas and the soups and the pasta sauces – Sardina swaying in the baby seat and Coco running ahead. He hung a right at the Deli Counter and into the Bakery Section. He looked left. He looked right. 'Coco?' he yelped. 'Where are you?' He dodged a baguette as it shot past his shoulder and struck the mayor's ear. A farmhouse loaf came sailing over his head, then a shower of crusty rolls.

'Get lost, slime-ball!' Coco roared. Out she darted from Cakes & Pastries with an apple pie in her hand. 'Jack,' she

hissed, 'head for the cornflakes – I'll stall the mayor with this!'

Jack scooted the trolley down Dry Goods: crisps . . . crackers . . . biscuits . . . breakfast cereals . . . *A-ha!* He glanced over his shoulder. *Come on, Coco – hurry!*

'What a sweet dog,' said a woman with frizzy hair. She popped a packet of cornflakes in her basket and reached out to pat Sardina's head. 'He's very unusual – what's his name?'

Sardina narrowed her eyes.

'Er . . .'

'Hey, Michael,' she called, 'come and have a look at this!'

A tall, skinny man with a net of oranges trotted down the aisle towards her. *Hurry, Coco – please!* Jack began to back away, dragging the trolley with him.

'Isn't it funny?' she was saying. 'Just over there – in that boy's shopping trolley.'

Uh-oh. Now a little girl was coming to have a look. Back he dragged the trolley –

back, back, back – and with a nifty swerve, he cut through to Household & Laundry. *Where is she? What's she doing?*

'Jack!'

'Coco!'

She was pounding down the aisle with the mayor hot on her heels. 'The check-outs,' she gasped. 'Run!'

Ratter-clat-clat – Jack swung to the right and charged to the front of the shop. 'There's a queue,' he wailed.

'Push in, you numb-bum!'

'I can't do that – it's rude.' *Ratter-clat-clat* – he swung to the left, Mayor Gristle just behind him, huffing and panting and wheezing. *He's getting louder. He's getting closer.* Jack felt the mayor's hairy fingers brush against his neck – he jerked his arm away as they groped at his sleeve, his throat tightened as they hooked inside his collar. 'Urrgh,' he gurgled, as Coco whizzed past. He staggered to a halt, gasping for breath. Mayor Gristle had him.

'The game's up,' the mayor growled, his fingers digging into Jack's shoulder. 'Let the trolley go and hand the walrus over.'

'Nnggh!' Jack spluttered.

Sardina was cowering under her flipper, trembling like a jelly in an earthquake.

'Not so fast!' Coco was standing before them, with a family-size bottle of cola in her hands. 'Get your hands off him, Gorilla-Pants!' She shook the bottle. *Psschtt!* She twisted the lid, stopped it with her thumb and aimed it at the mayor. 'I said let him go or . . .'

'Or what?' spat Mayor Gristle.

'Or your face is going for a wash, rinse and spin.'

'You wouldn't dare,' he snarled. 'I'm the Mayor of . . .'

WHOOSH! His head vanished in a flash of brown spray.

'Arf-arf!' Sardina lunged and batted him with her flipper.

Ratter-clat-clat – along the row of tills Jack galloped. 'Out the way!' he bellowed. Left – right – left, people staggering sideways as he swerved through the queues. Coco snatched up a bag of flour and hurled it over her shoulder.

BOOF! The aisle dissolved in an explosion of white. 'Wow,' she breathed. 'It's like Christmas.'

'Come *on,* Coco – move it!' He crashed through an empty checkout and headed for the exit. He could see the High Street through the glass doors – the bus stop, the traffic, the car park and – Snivell! He was standing by the trolley bay dusting off his cap. Jack stopped. He swerved.

'Arf–arf–arf!'

Back he went again – *ratter-clat-clat* – Pet Food . . . Detergents . . . Stationery & Back to School. He slammed to a stop. Wines & Spirits. Rows and rows of bottles stacked against the wall.

'It's a dead end, Coco – we can't go any further. We're doomed – we're done for – we're . . .'

'The fire exit,' she cried. 'Follow that sign!'

TWENTY-TWO

Jack and Coco clattered the trolley across the car park and over the street to the bus stop. The number 52 was leaving.

'WAIT!' yelled Jack, rapping on its doors. 'Open up!' He glanced over his shoulder: Mayor Gristle was careering across the road, steam blasting from his ears like a volcano about to blow. *Rap-rap-rap.* '*Plee-ase.*' The driver looked round and – *woomph* – the doors swung open. 'Thank you,' said Jack, tipping Sardina out of the trolley. 'Thank you so much. Thank you so, so, so, so much.'

'What's that hairy thing?' said the driver.

'That's my friend, Coco.'

'Not her. *That.*' He nodded towards Sardina. She nodded back and hauled herself through the door.

'She's a short-haired Sardine Terrier,' said Coco. 'Don't worry, she's bus-trained.' She reached into her backpack and dropped some coins in the tray.

'Phew — that was close.' Jack sank into the back seat next to Coco and Sardina. 'I really thought he had me there — he practically ruptured my jugular.'

'Admit it,' said Coco, 'it was the best fun

ever. Did you see his face when I shot him with the cola gun?'

'*Shh!*' Jack nodded to the front of the bus. 'It's *him!*'

'Where?' She peered over the top of the seat and giggled. 'He looks like something the cat sicked up.'

The mayor was standing in the doorway shouting at the bus driver, the seat of his trousers flapping in the breeze. His moustache and eyebrows were dusted white and a carrot shaving dangled from his nose. 'I'm the Mayor of Curtly Ambrose. I order you to let me on!'

'And I'm the King of Cuckoo-Land. No ticket, no travel.'

'I don't want to travel, you buffoon – I

want to retrieve my walrus!'

'Oh yeah . . .' the driver sighed. 'That's what they all say. But if you don't buy a ticket you can't come on board.'

'All right, I'll pay.' He slammed his briefcase on to the tray and flicked it open. 'But you haven't heard the last of this.'

A dead mackerel flopped out of the briefcase.

'This your idea of a joke?' said the driver, as it slithered over the tray and into his lap. 'You've got two seconds to get off my bus or I'm calling the police.'

Woomph! – the doors slammed shut. The traffic lights turned green, the bus pulled away from the stop and left Mayor Gristle by the side of the road.

TWENTY-THREE

'Not *again*,' said Jack, as the number 52 glided to a halt outside the Deja-View Cinema. 'If this bus went any slower we'd go into reverse. How long are we stopping for now?' He scanned the passengers queuing to board, then twisted around to look out the back. 'Come on, come on, come *on*.'

Woomph — the doors swung open. The back seat was filling up now: a bent old lady in a straw hat and a tartan shawl . . . two teenage girls . . . a young woman with a red umbrella.

'Can't you sit still for two seconds?' said Coco. 'You're making me jumpy.'

'Something doesn't feel right,' he whispered. 'I'm so spooked out I can even *smell* him.' He shuddered. 'Dead mackerel and mayonnaise – it's like Mayor Gristle's sitting right next to me.'

'It's over, Jack – he's miles away. And anyway, there's no way the driver'll let him on now.'

The bus pulled out again – past the church … a florist's … a Chinese takeaway …

'So what now?' said Jack, his fingers drumming on his knee. 'Where are we going exactly?'

'This bus stops at the station. We'll have to change for the zoo.'

'I told you. Sardina's not from the zoo – I drew her.'

'Don't talk cow-splat.'

'I *did* – I found a feather in my desk and I –'

'A *feather*?'

'A feather with ink inside. It was magic, Coco – whatever I drew just appeared – zap – out of nowhere. Like the bluebottles and The Ravioli Ultra and Sardina and the fish and – and . . .'

'And your frilly knickers,' said Coco.

'And my frill— and my wrestling mask.' Jack stared out of the window: they were turning off a roundabout and chugging up a hill. 'And then Itch took it . . .'

'The big guy?'

Jack nodded. Now they were driving past the park.

'Jack . . .' said Coco, as she delved into her backpack.

'Hmm?' Past the swings and a roundabout . . . pigeons . . . a spotty dog . . . two goalposts in a muddy field . . .

'Jack, you numb-sock – is this it?'

'I . . . I don't believe it!' There was the feather – in her hand – lighting her face like a hundred birthday candles. 'How . . . ? Where . . . ? How – how come?'

'Me and Sardina were waiting for you outside your house, remember? By the car? You were taking ages. Then Itch came out with your desk on his shoulder and it fell out on the pavement and he didn't even notice.' She shrugged. 'So I kept it.'

'Quick,' said Jack, as he reached for his feather. 'Have you got any paper in your bag?'

Jack filled the bottom of the page with circles.

'What are they?' said Coco.

'Pebbles.'

'If you say so.'

He drew a line across with squiggles underneath.

'And what's that?'

'It's the horizon, okay? And that's the sea and will you please stop asking questions because you've already made me go wrong.'

'Just change that wobbly bit into a rock,' she said. 'Anyway, what happens now?'

'Just you wait.' He slid the feather back into Coco's backpack, folded his arms and sat back. *Hope it doesn't flood the bus.*

Coco looked at the picture. She twizzled her pigtail. She coughed, she frowned, she hummed a bit and she looked at the picture again. 'Looks like it hasn't worked.'

'Oh, it'll work all right.'

'Maybe it's run out of magic.' She thrust her chin into her hand and tapped her foot. 'Come on Jack, let's take her to the zoo.'

'When will you get it into your fruit-filled brain – she doesn't come from the –'

The bus shuddered to a halt. 'Everybody off!' called the driver.

Sardina flung herself at the window, her flippers flat on the glass. 'Arf-arf-arf!'

'What's got into her?' said Coco.

'This isn't the station!' said a man with a suitcase.

'Er — special stop,' said the driver, reaching for his map.

'Where's McCluskey's Toy Shop gone?' asked a man holding a little boy's hand.

'Must've taken a wrong turn,' the driver muttered, tracing the map with his finger. 'Everybody off! Go and stretch your legs while I get this sorted.'

'What are we waiting for?' said Jack. 'Let's go!'

tWENtY-FOUR

'Well, I'll be jiggered!' said the man with the suitcase, heaving it off the bus. 'I never knew Curtly Ambrose was by the sea.' The passengers were wandering here and there across the beach, scratching their heads. Seagulls wheeled overhead and the sea glittered under a cloudless sky.

'Grandad?' said the little boy, crouching on the sand. 'What are these?'

'Most peculiar . . .' he said. 'They look like baked potatoes.'

'I don't believe it!' Coco squinted at the horizon where a wobbly rock jutted out of the water. '*You* did it!'

Jack breathed deep; he could taste the tingle of salt on his tongue and he smiled. *I did it, all right.*

'So it's true.' Coco turned to him, cheeks pink and eyes shining. 'The magic feather's true! And I thought it was one of your –'

'Hey!' the young woman was calling. 'Has anyone seen my umbrella?'

Jack frowned. He was watching Sardina lolloping down the beach.

'My red umbrella – it's gone!'

What were those clothes by the water's edge? Jack stood on his tiptoes, shielding his eyes with his hand: a tartan shawl . . . a yellow hat . . . He gulped. A black suit, a white shirt and a pair of shiny pointed shoes. 'Oh no.' He grabbed Coco's arm. 'Oh no, oh no, oh no.'

'You okay? You've gone blotchy again. Hey! Where are you going?'

Jack was running down the beach now, slipping over the sand and stumbling over the baked potatoes. He skidded to a halt at the water's edge. 'SARDINA!' he yelled, as she plunged into the surf. 'WAIT!'

Coco ran after him, panting as she reached the shoreline. 'Stop doing that, will you? You're always running off and acting weird.'

'Come back!' His voice cracked as the water closed over Sardina's tail. '*Please*,' he rasped. 'Come back.'

Coco grabbed him by the arm as he

staggered towards the water. 'What's the big deal? She's only having a swim.'

'That smell on the bus . . . the old lady sitting next to us . . .' With a trembling finger he pointed at the pile of clothes on the sand. 'It was him all along.'

'Who? Mayor Gristle?' She giggled. 'You actually think he's in the sea? Don't be daft, Jack –'

WHOOSH! Out of the ocean he reared: the Mayor of Curtly Ambrose – metres from where they stood.

'Hah!' He bared his yellow teeth and lunged back into the spray. 'Arf-arf!'

Into the air he flung Sardina: a twist of black – a flash of red umbrella – then down she sank like stone.

'No,' Jack wailed. 'No – please – no!'

'Surprise!' spluttered Mayor Gristle, standing waist-deep in the sea. Water streamed over his bulging belly and his gold chain glinted through the hairs on his chest. *Heuurcch!* He hacked up a gobbet of seawater and wiped the slime off his chin with his arm.

'Thought you'd seen the last of me, eh? Well, think again, losers.' With a jerk he yanked up Sardina's head, caught in the crook of the red umbrella. 'Say hello to Wally!'

'Harf!' she coughed. 'Harf-harf!'

'Stop hurting her,' yelled Coco. 'And she's called Sardina, you dumb-bum!'

'Keep your mouth shut, missy, or I'll hurt

it some more.' And he gave the umbrella a twist.

'Ar-*whoooo*!' Sardina's howl rang out across the water.

'We'll behave,' cried Jack. 'We'll do anything you want!'

'That's more like it.' Mayor Gristle licked his lips. 'I want to see what this magic feather can do.'

'*What?*'

'I know your secret, Jackie boy – I was on the bus, remember? Now let me see . . .' He tweaked his moustache. His piggy eyes lit up. 'A yacht! That's it – I want you to draw me a super-yacht like all the celebrities have.'

'A *super-yacht*? But I'm no good at

drawing. I – I don't know how they go!'

'Don't give me that – I want a yacht and I want the works: racing sails and power steering and a sun deck for photo opportunities!'

Jack slumped on to the shingle and with a trembling hand he started to draw. He drew a big semi-circle and three triangles. He drew a long thin line – and another and another.

'Ar-*whoooo!*'

'Hurry,' said Coco. 'He's pulling her whiskers!'

He drew parabolas, cubes, cylinders, circles, rectangles, cones and squares.

'Get a move on, Jack – *please.*'

'I'm trying. I'm trying.' He drew a criss-cross for a steering wheel and then he shut the pad. 'I'm done.'

He closed his eyes and swallowed.

WHOOOOOSH! CLANG!

'Hmmm . . .' said Mayor Gristle. 'I see what you mean about the drawing. Don't they teach you anything at school?'

There bobbed the yacht on the calm blue sea, just behind the mayor: it had thirteen radar dishes poking up like mushrooms and a forest of masts of all different lengths; it had three sails: one big, one small and one slightly square; it had rigging and funnels, a sloping sun-deck and seventeen anchors dangling from its rickety rails.

'Never mind,' said the mayor. 'The feather works and that's what counts. Now, Jackie boy – take off your shoes.'

'I – I don't understand.'

'You're going to wade out and give me the feather, you sludge brain.' He stared out across the beach with distant eyes. 'The magic feather – I'll be rich at last! I'll draw a palace in the High Street – gold taps . . . marble floors . . . and a statue of me in the garden, fifty metres tall. I'll change my name to President Gristle and name the town after me!' He stroked his moustache. 'Yes . . . Gristletown – I like it.' The piggy eyes snapped back. 'Bring it to me now,' he roared, 'or I'll turn the walrus into burgers!'

Give him my feather . . . My magic feather? But he's madder than a bag of spanners. Jack breathed in deep. *What do I do? Think, think, think.* He scooped up a handful of

sand and let it fall through his fingers. *A-ha!*
Jack smiled a tiny smile. *Maybe, he thought,*
just maybe . . .

tWENtY-FIVE

Jack kicked off his trainers, rolled up his jeans and pulled his scarf and t-shirt off. He unclipped his Viking helmet and laid it at the water's edge. With one last glance at the clear blue sky, he slid his goggles over his eyes and into the sea he waded, holding the feather high above his head. Deeper and deeper he went, till the waves lapped at his chin.

'It's covered in sand, you idiot boy!' Mayor Gristle snatched the feather and clasped it to his hairy chest. 'At last,' he said, his lower lip quivering. 'The magic feather's mine!'

'Will you let Sardina go now?'

'Let Sardina go? Did you say: *Let Sardina go?* My poor young fellow – you must have a screw loose.'

'You . . . you can't do this!' Coco yelled, as Mayor Gristle clambered on to his yacht, hauling Sardina up by her neck with a yank of the umbrella.

'Oh, yes I can.' He stood dripping on the deck, his hairy belly hanging over his polka-dot underpants. 'I'm the Mayor of Curtly Ambrose. I can do anything I like.'

I wouldn't be so sure . . . thought Jack.

'Don't you even care?' Coco turned to Jack, tears rolling down her freckled cheeks. 'What are you smiling for? You heard him . . . he'll turn her into burgers!'

'See that shiny thing on side of the boat?'

She sniffed and nodded and wiped her eyes.

'Just you wait. Any second now and . . .'

'**AAAAARGH!**' screamed the mayor. 'You leave my wing mirror alone!'

Clank!

'You're trashing my vessel, you hooligan!'

KERCHANG!

'That's my digital sextant. If you touch

my life jacket, you'll walk the plank!'

Rrr-i-pp! Scraps of polystyrene and orange plastic hit the water and bobbed away.

'That does it – you're off!' Mayor Gristle heaved Sardina towards the rail and hurled her overboard. ***SPLASH!*** He strode into the cabin, grumbling and muttering and – '**AAAAARGH!**' – he was back on the deck. 'Hey, you!' he called to shore. 'Where's the engine on this thing?'

'Whoops!' Jack scratched his head. 'I always forget the bit, don't I Coco?'

'*What?*'

'There isn't an engine. And there isn't a rudder either.'

'You gormless twerp – you think

you can fool me? Haven't you forgotten something?' He waved the feather in the air. 'I'll draw it myself!'

'Jack . . . ?' said Coco, peeking into her backpack. 'Is this what I think it is?'

'Uh-huh.'

'You kept it all along!' Her face glowed as she pulled the magic feather out. 'I don't get it – what did you give to Mayor Gristle?'

'Oh that?' Jack grinned. 'Just some old seagull feather. I found it in the sand.'

tWENtY-SIX

'Can't you draw the waves a bit bigger?' said Coco. 'And maybe add a shark or two?'

'Keep your freckled nose out of it,' said Jack, as he guided the feather-tip over the page. 'I'm trying to concentrate.'

'Whoopsie.'

'I don't believe it – you've done it again.' He peered at his drawing. 'There's a massive streak in the sky now.'

'It's only a bit of wind.' Coco licked her finger and tried to rub it out.

'Stop smudging it, will you? You'll turn

it into a tornado.'

'It's run out of ink!' Mayor Gristle hollered from the deck. 'How do I get this blinking feather to work?'

Coco cupped her hands round her mouth. 'You have to say the magic word!'

'What is it, you pestilential creature? I command you to tell me this instant.'

'Now, let me think . . .' She twizzled her pigtail. 'Nope – I've forgotten.'

'Forgotten? You idiot girl, how can you forget the magic word?' He hoisted up his underpants as the yacht rocked to and fro. 'I know your game, but you can't stop me – I'll try every magic word there is.' He stamped his foot. 'Abracadabra!' He clicked his fingers. 'Alakazam!'

The breeze was picking up; a cloud scudded over the sun and the sea began to swell. Up heaved the yacht, then down it plunged. Up – up – up – then down. *Ye-ss!* thought Jack. *It's working.* He pulled his scarf around his ears as the wind whistled around him.

'Open sesame!' bawled Mayor Gristle, gripping on to the deck rails. 'Monosodium Glutamate!' The yacht pitched sideways and across the deck he staggered. 'Gazpacho!' he shrieked, as the yacht swept out to the open sea. Up – up – up – then down. 'Hey presto!…

Contact lens!'

'I'm freezing,' said Coco. She wrapped her arms around herself and grinned. 'Hey – look who's back!'

About ten metres out a whiskery head was gliding over the rolling waves.

'Sardina! Over here!' Jack jumped up and down and waved his scarf in the air. 'She's turning her head – she's seen us.' Up she went – then down again. Up – up – up – then down. 'She's never swum in the sea before. D'you think she'll be okay?'

'She'll be fine, Jack – look!' One . . . two . . . three whiskery heads popped up around Sardina. 'Oh, she's going to have so much fun – she's already making friends!'

Far in the distance, the Mayor of Curtly Ambrose was heading for the wobbly rock, a fleck of black against the silver sea. 'Ambidextrous!' he called. 'In-growing toenail!' The yacht dipped over the horizon and his cries were lost on the wind.

One . . . two . . . three whiskery heads sank below the surface.

'She's the last one left,' said Jack. 'See her flipper? She's waving at us. I . . . I think she's saying goodbye.'

'Arf–arf!'

'Goodbye,' he called. 'Good luck!'

Sardina did a backward flip and re-emerged with a yellow ball in her mouth. She flicked it up with her nose and, with a swipe of her flipper, she batted it on to the beach. The wind dropped. The black clouds melted into the blue.

Jack blinked and rubbed his eyes. And then
Sardina was gone.

tWENtY-SEVEN

WOOMPH! – the doors slammed shut, the motor revved and – *chug-chug-chug* – the bus pulled away from the beach.

Coco settled into the back seat and grinned. 'D'you know something?' she said, 'You weren't half bad . . . for a Scaredy Sock.'

'It was nothing. Just call me Jumping Jack Dangerous.'

He sat back, folded his arms and looked around the bus: the man with his suitcase . . . the two teenage girls . . . the small boy just in front and his grandad reading the paper. He smiled to himself. *Do they actually realise there's a hero on board?* He closed his eyes and pictured the headlines: *Gristle No Match for Schoolboy Muscle . . . Superhero Saves the Town . . . Awarded a Lifetime Supply of Caramel Smoothies . . .*

'Jack?'

'M–hm?'

Coco nudged him with her elbow. 'Jack, you lame brain – wake up!'

He opened his eyes: they were pulling into a bus stop. The grandad and the little boy were getting up to leave. He yawned. 'What d'you want now?'

'Your dad,' she hissed. 'His photo's in the paper.'

'Not now Coco, I'm tired.'

'He's made the headlines.' She grabbed the newspaper from the seat in front. '*Hopes Dashed*,' she read. '*Mayor Fights Off Savage Walrus.*'

'*What?*' Jack sat up. He snatched the paper from her. There it was: a photo of his father on the front page of the *Curtly Ambrose Evening Echo*. He scanned the story underneath: *exclusive interview with chief witness, Vernon Snivell . . . 'new employee set the wild beast upon him . . . lacerations to his throat and vital organs . . . we had no choice . . . sack Mr Dash . . .' Mayor Gristle unavailable for comment . . .* 'I don't believe it!' he spluttered. 'That's not what happened. Every single word is a stinky rotten lie!'

'So he lied,' said Coco. 'Who cares? The

mayor's gone now. We beat him in the end.'

'No. We didn't. Don't you see? He beat us.'

'What are you on about? He's lost at sea in a pair of spotty underpants!'

'They sacked my dad. And it's all my fault. If I hadn't found the feather and I hadn't drawn Sardina and she hadn't bitten the mayor and ... and ...' Jack flung his head in his arms. 'I was s'posed to be on my best behaviour. I was s'posed to make them proud.'

'Don't worry. It'll be okay in a couple of days, you'll see. My dad went ballistic when I built a swimming pool in my bedroom, but he was fine once the carpet dried out.'

'This is a zillion times worse than a soggy carpet – my dad's lost his job and it's all over the papers. His photo's on the front page – it's a national scandal! What am I gonna do?'

But Coco was gazing out of the window, twizzling her pigtail and humming to herself.

†WEN†Y-EIGH†

'Come on, dozy knickers, this is our stop.'

Jack climbed off the bus and turned to look up Quarantine Street. The sun was sinking behind the rooftops and striping the street with shadows. He stood on his toes and squinted into the distance: he could just see his house at the top of the hill. The knot in his stomach tightened.

'I feel sick,' he said, as they trudged up the hill.

'You look it.'

He shook his head. 'I just don't get it.'

'Get what?'

'The magic feather. What's the point in having it when it just gets me into trouble?' He sighed. 'I wish I could make it all better . . . but I can't exactly draw my dad's job back.'

'Nearly there,' said Coco, as they reached the post box. 'I'm going home for a peanut butter sandwich. See you tomorrow, okay?'

Jack tried to answer, but his mouth had gone dry. He swallowed and reached for the doorbell.

tWENtY-NINE

'I'm sure there's nothing to worry about,' said Mum. 'Dad will find another job. He's a very clever man.' She sat down at the kitchen table. 'We can always sell a few things . . . like the fridge and the car . . . the doorbell and my new tiara.'

'So where is he?' said Jack.

'Mmmmm?' She was gazing into the distance, dabbing her eyes with a hanky.

'Mum . . . ? Where's Dad gone?'

'The Town Hall. They called him in. It's that silly business with the walrus,' she said, waving her hand in the air. 'They want to ask him some questions.' Her face crumpled. 'Oh dumpling!' she wailed, 'they might press charges!'

'W-what d'you mean?'

'Police cars . . . handcuffs . . . that sort of thing.' She picked up a photo from the kitchen table. 'Look at us . . .' She sniffed. 'We used to be so happy!' Her head disappeared into her hanky. Her shoulders heaved and the photo fell from her hand.

Jumping Jack Dangerous, what have you done? He dropped his head. *It's all my fault and there's nothing I can do.* His eyes fell on the photo. He felt his heart flutter. *Or maybe . . . just maybe there is . . .*

'Mum?' he said, 'I need a pencil. It's an emergency!'

Jack picked up a note off his desk.

Returned: one desk of wooden construction. All woodworm, weevils, termites, beetles, ants and silverfish treated, exterminated and eradicated.

Returned: one pest-free leather-bound volume found inside the above, containing a number of drawings of questionable merit (apart from the rubbish skip on roller skates, which was quite good).

Kind regards,

Itch and Scratchett,

Verminators to the Queen

Jack sat down and opened the book at an empty page and laid the photo beside it. *I'll copy it out in pencil first so I don't make any mistakes.* Up, along and down – he drew the outline of the house with a triangle on top for the roof. He drew five squares for the windows and an oblong for the door and above it he wrote number 7. He drew three front steps and a wonky gate . . . Dad in his glasses and Mum in her tiara . . . and in between them he drew himself.

This is it. Boom – boom – boom – he could feel his heart pounding. *I'll trace it with the feather and – zap – we're going home!*

'Okay . . .' he said, peeking under the book, 'so where is it?' He lifted the lid and looked inside. *Uh-oh!* He checked on the floor and

under his chair. 'Arrrrgh! I don't believe it —
the Fruitcake's still got it in her . . .'

Bam! The bedroom door flew open.
'Guess what?' said Coco. 'You forgot your
feather, you numb-bum!'

'What d'you mean? It was in your
backpack and you walked right off with
it. There's a word for that, Coco — and it's
daylight muggery!'

'Give it a rest, Grandma — I've got to
be quick. I snuck out while my dad was at
the shops.' She shuffled off her backpack
and sat on the bed. 'Ooh — this is nice!' she
said, bouncing up and down. 'New rug . . .
new curtains . . . Shame about the same old
manky desk.'

'Just hand it over, will you?'

'Don't get your pants in a pickle – I have to find it first.' She plunged in her arm and rummaged inside. 'And you better not use it without me. I'll come round tomorrow after breakfast, okay?'

'Er – about tomorrow . . .'

'Oh, I can't wait!' A ball of string fell out of her backpack and rolled on to the floor. 'We're going to have so much fun!'

'Thing is . . .' said Jack, scratching his eyebrow, 'I'm busy after breakfast.'

'Zero problemo. I'll come round after lunch.' She pulled out a plastic frog and dropped it on to the bed. 'Now where is it . . . ? I know I packed it . . .'

'Actually,' he said, 'I'm busy all day. I'm having my toenails clipped.'

'Must be in here somewhere . . .' she
said, tipping her bag out on to the duvet.
'Ah, here it is!'

Jack swallowed. 'Coco . . . I need to tell
you something.'

'Oh no!' Up she jumped. 'My dad's

going to *kill* me.' She slung her backpack over her shoulder and headed for the door. 'See you tomorrow – got to go.'

'Coco – wait! You've forgotten your stuff.'

'He'll be back any minute,' she called from the landing, 'and I've left his slippers in the toaster.'

'But I ...' *Thump-thump-thump* – she was running down the stairs. 'But I wanted to say goodbye.'

Jack sat down. He looked at his feather, shining on the duvet – at the bits and pieces scattered all around. He smiled: two bus tickets . . . the rear-view mirror . . . one baked potato and a crusty roll . . . a newspaper folded in half . . . He picked up the newspaper and smoothed it on to his knee. *It's the front page of the Evening Echo . . .*

'Dumpling?'

Mum! She was standing in the doorway, wild-eyed and panting. 'I've ordered a pizza delivery to celebrate!'

'Huh?'

'Dad just phoned. Isn't it wonderful?'

'Mum – what are you . . . ?'

She clapped her hand to her mouth and giggled. 'He's even got a gold chain!' And then she slammed the door.

Uh-oh. Mum's lost it big time. The sooner we get out of here the better. He lifted the newspaper off his knee. *Better get on with it, I s'pose . . .* He blinked. 'I don't believe it . . .' He rubbed his eyes.

'Now that's clever, Coco. Very, very clever.' Jack got up and went to his desk. He took one last look at his pencil drawing and then he closed the book. A slow smile spread across his face. 'Maybe you're not such a fruitcake after all.'

PENCILS & MAGIC FEATHERS At tHE READY!

LEt's DO SOME DRAWING!

(WItH A LIttLE HELP FROM toP ILLUSTRAtOR, JUDY BROWN.)

EVER WONDERED HOW to DRAW...

A HAPPY SEA LION?
HERE'S HOW:

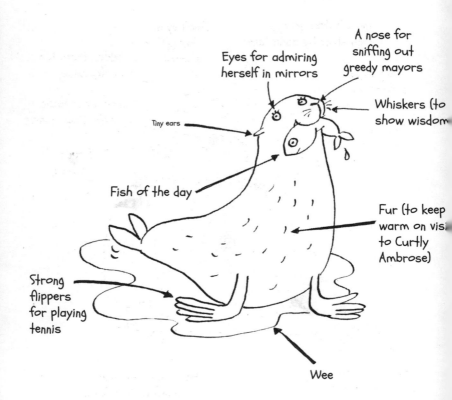

OR AN ANGRY MAYOR?
HERE'S HOW:

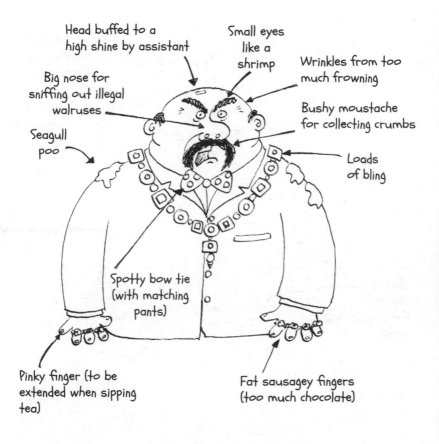

TRY IT YOURSELF!

ABOUT THE AUTHOR:

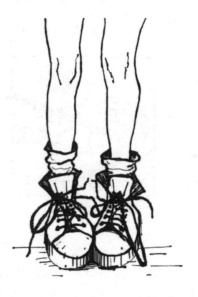

Sophie Plowden is five foot eleven
and three quarters.

She likes painting and writing
and teaching art. And salted liquorice.

ABOUT THE ILLUSTRATOR:

Judy Brown has been drawing pictures
(and writing stories) for as long as
she can remember.

She has three children
and lives in Surrey with her illustrator
husband and two stroppy brown cats.

ACKNOWLEDGEMENTS

I'd like to thank everyone who brought this book to life: my parents, my friends and family, Ben Illis, my agent, and Liz Bankes, my editor – and Judy Brown, who knows where to draw the line.

COMING IN 2016!

JACK DASH AND THE SUMMER BLIZZARD...

Jack thought back to the creepy nightmare he'd had the night before and shivered. *It's something to do with the feather – I'm sure.*

'Guess what?' said Coco, as they set off down Quarantine Street in the morning sunshine. 'I've got it.'

'Got what?' said Jack.

'The feather. It's in my backpack.'

'My magic feather?' Jack stopped walking. He gawped at Coco; his cheeks were burning. 'You're . . . you're joking, right?'

'Nope. I found it in your bedroom.'

'You went into my *bedroom?*'

'Yep — it was easy. I ran upstairs when your mum was banging on and there it was — under your bed, hidden in a football sock and locked in a box. First place I looked.' She shuffled off her backpack, dumped it on the pavement and rubbed her palms together.

'Hang on!' said Jack, 'I happen to possess the most remarkable supernatural phenomenon known to humankind and you want to get it out and use it? Here? In the middle of Quarantine Street? No way, Coco. Not in a billion light years.'

'Who cares where we are? It's gonna be even more fun than cutting my dad's hair. And anyway, I already drew something.'

'Harrk!'

Jack stiffened. 'What was that?' he said, looking up and down the street.

'*Hah – aarrk!*'

'Blinking Noreen – it's coming from in there!' He pointed at her backpack sitting at her feet. 'What's inside that thing, Coco?' He took a step back. 'D–did you see that? It's *moving!*'

Backwards and forwards rocked the bag, then over it toppled, onto the pavement; something black and shiny was pushing up the flap.

'It's alive,' Jack squawked, 'and it's trying to get out!'

FOR MORE LAUGH OUT LOUD FUNNY BOOKS FOLLOW THE CAT!

JACK D

AHEM... FOLLOW THE **CAT...** (*NOT* THE PIG)

www.catnippublishing.co.uk
Twitter: @catnipbooks